Golden Wings & Pretty Things

KAYLEIGH KING

Copyright © 2022 by Kayleigh King

All rights reserved.

No part of this book may be reproduced in any form or by any electronic or mechanical means, including information storage and retrieval systems, without written permission from the author, except for the use of brief quotations in a book review.

This is a work of fiction. Names, characters, businesses, places, events, locales, and incidents are either the products of the author's imagination or used in a fictitious manner. Any resemblance to actual persons, living or dead, or actual events is purely coincidental.

Cover Design: Cat Imb at TRC DESIGNS

Copy Editing: Ellie McLove MY BROTHER'S EDITOR

Copy Editing: Amanda Rash DRAFT HOUSE EDITORIAL SERVICES

Proof Reading: Rosa Sharon MY BROTHER'S EDITOR

ISBN: 978-1-7359304-9-7

BLURB

I don't often deny myself. If I want it, I'll find a way to obtain it, not caring what lines I have to cross.
She is the exception.
Indie is forbidden, a toy that isn't mine to break but she is a pretty thing I'm eager to play with.
For months I've tried to resist and keep my distance.
But it would appear the fates are finally on my side because now she's willingly come to *me*.
She's in trouble and I'm the only one who can help… that is if she's willing to pay the price.
I want everything, and I'll accept nothing less from her.
She walked into my life on the arm of my son, but I intend to keep her for myself.

A NOTE FROM THE AUTHOR

TRIGGER WARNING - Please Read:

Golden Wings & Pretty Things is an age gap/boyfriend's father romance that includes themes of coercion, cheating (not on each other but with each other), sexually explicit scenes and strong language. It may not be suitable for readers under the age of eighteen.

NOTE: Astor and Indie's story acts as the prequel for the author's upcoming series, *Fractured Rhymes*. The first thirteen chapters were originally included in the *Bully God Anthology* (Published 02.22.22), but it is encouraged that readers start from the beginning again as some names/timelines have changed.

For those who go after what they want without shame or hesitation.

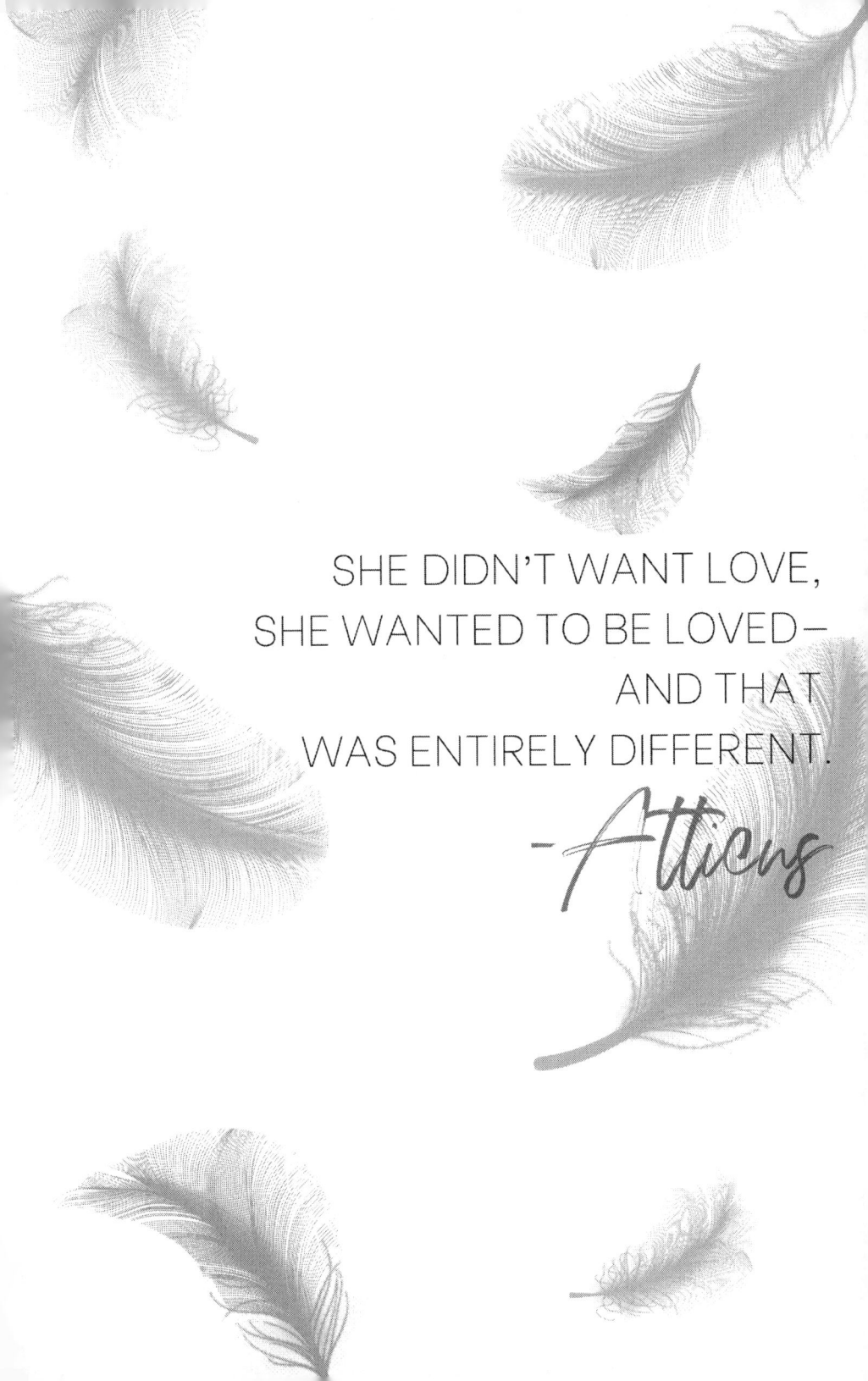

SHE DIDN'T WANT LOVE,
SHE WANTED TO BE LOVED—
AND THAT
WAS ENTIRELY DIFFERENT.

—Atticus

PLAYLIST

Listen to the whole playlist at spoti.fi/**3a0aMDZ**

Break My Baby - KALEO
She Treats Me Well - Ben Howard
Hollow - Will Champlin
Steady Love - Evergreen
Love Like Ours - Aron Wright
Tsunami - FLØRE
White Doves - Kyla La Grange
Wings - Birdy
Lose Ourselves - Boundary Run
Whenever You're Around - Bootstraps
All I Want - Daniella Mason
Dreams - Caroline Glaser
I Don't Want to Let You Go - Jordan Hart

ONE
INDIE
JULY

"WATCH OUT!" is the only warning I get before ice cold water splashes across my skin, stunning me out of the relaxed state I'd found myself in. The group erupts into laughter and cheers as I fly up into a sitting position on the large inflatable dock just in time to watch Callan's head resurface.

His perfectly straight teeth flash when he finds me gaping at him in shock. "Did I get you?"

This causes even more laughter from our friends, who either lie on the dock with me or float on smaller colorful rafts all around us. Callan is the only one fully submerged in the frigid water. It may be July, but Lake Washington never gets much above sixty-five degrees.

I look down at my now waterlogged yellow bikini and back at my boyfriend. "Maybe just a little bit." It takes effort to keep my face pulled in a scowl, a smile and laugh fighting to the surface.

Callan sees right through it though. "Only a little bit?" His muscular arms, tan from spending our summer on the lake, glide with ease through the water. He stops just feet in front of me, his dark blue eyes searching me over. "Show me where I missed.

I'm going to need to get there too," he taunts, his lips pulling into a smug smirk.

It's refreshing to see Callan like this. He's been so serious lately. I've tried asking him about it, but he's been cagey and vague with his answers. The desire to push him on it is strong, but when people pry me for information, it makes me want to punch them in the nose. So, I've tried my best to be patient.

He'll tell me when he's ready. Or at least I hope he will.

It's always been a toss-up with Callan. Since the beginning, it's felt like he's been holding back.

His hand wraps around my ankle, and with a harsh pull, he yanks me dangerously close to the edge. My nails dig into the surface to try and prevent him from pulling me further. I have a feeling it's in vain though. My legs now dangle in the chilly water, making goosebumps dance across my skin.

"How about a quick dip, Indie?" Callan takes my other ankle in his grasp too. "Just so we can get all the places I missed."

"Don't you dare," I warn, my smile still threatening to escape no matter how much I don't want to get back in the lake. It took thirty minutes of laying in the sun to finally warm myself up after my brisk swim out here. Shore isn't far, forty feet at most, but it feels a lot farther when your muscles seize up from the icy water.

"Wouldn't dream of it. I promise." Callan lifts my foot out of the lake, bringing it to his mouth. He presses a kiss to the arch, his eyes locked with mine while he does.

It's a sweet moment he completely ruins by breaking his promise.

There's barely enough time for me to release a startled yelp before I'm fully submerged. The abrupt change in temperature is a shock to the system. My body stiffens and my chest aches.

It's only a few seconds I'm under, but it feels like minutes.

Not once do Callan's hands leave my body as he pulls me up

and I surface, making a screeching sound. *"Holy shit!"* I shriek once I've sucked in a breath.

My boyfriend's laugh fills my ears while I shove the hair that's stuck to my forehead back. "Look how fast you get wet for me," he muses.

His hands flex on my hips and a shiver of anticipation shoots through me. It's been too long since we've slept together, and I miss being touched. In addition to his new evasive demeanor, he's been coming over less and less. When he does, he doesn't spend the night.

Since summer break started, he hasn't invited me over to his place on campus either. Before, there were times I spent two weeks there, not once returning to my own apartment. When we first got together almost six months ago, it was all heat. Didn't matter where we were, Callan's hands were on me, but now, I feel like I have to *work* to get him to show interest in me. And I'm starting to grow tired.

The red flags are basically glowing neon signs at this point.

I'm wary, but still pleased by his change in attitude now. I don't even care that our friends are five feet away from us, possibly eavesdropping.

"*Mmmhmm*," I agree, looping my arms around his neck, bringing our faces closer. "You got me wet, now what are you going to do about it?"

Callan's eyes flick to my lips, but where I should see desire reflected in them, all I find is contemplation.

Fuck this.

No longer waiting for him to make a move, I close the distance myself and test the waters.

I remember the first time Callan Banes kissed me. He literally swept me off my feet because he stole my ability to stand with a simple kiss. It was the epitome of making a girl weak in the knees. At the time, I thought that kiss was going to be my last first kiss.

Our kiss now confirms that I may have been wrong that night. Ever since then, I've been chasing that feeling like an addict chasing their first high. And now I'm starting to wonder if it's even worth it.

People sometimes describe kisses like a dance. There's passion and an elegant rhythm. The choreography should be exciting to perform. It feels taxing and boring now. Almost like it's a chore.

"Callan!" Hansen hollers from the dock I'd been yanked from, making Callan pull away. "Get your ass up here. I need a partner. Zadie and Lark think they have a chance against me in beer pong."

"Oh! I don't *think* anything," Zadie shouts back at Hansen from the hot pink raft she sits on. "I *know*. I saw how you threw the ball last week at practice. We have this in the bag." Her hand points at the floating beer pong table, the various bracelets she wears chime every time she moves. "I'll bet you two hundred dollars right now that us *girls* can kick your ass six ways from Sunday."

Zadie Hill looks like a sweet little pixie, but she can verbally destroy the strongest of men. It's one of my favorite things to witness.

"Hey!" Hansen shouts at her. "Don't be a bitch."

"I'm not a bitch, I'm a fucking lady," Zadie hurls the ball in her lap at him. He catches it with ease, causing a scowl to form. "Stop talking and let's play."

Callan laughs, his handsome face pulling into a huge smile. "You're on, Hill." His quick kiss on my cheek feels like a dismissal as he pushes away from me without a second thought.

I stay there treading water, watching him swim away, not really sure what I'm waiting for him to do. Come back? Ask me to join? Just...*something*.

It's Lark, the stunning, soft spoken, blonde with the kind

smile that yells over to me. Not my boyfriend. "Indie! Come on!" She motions me with her hand. "We can take turns."

I think over her offer for all of two seconds before I shake my head at her. "No, it's okay," I lie. "You guys go ahead. I need to go inside and see if my mom called me back."

Not a complete lie. I have an event this weekend and need to make sure that everything is still okay on her end. When I told Mom my wish to participate in this competition, she dragged her feet on giving me her blessing. I'm counting down the days till I no longer need her permission.

For three years, I've squirreled away every loose piece of change and dollar bill I don't need to live so I can finally buy Jupiter from her. It's ridiculous that I would have to do such a thing when my dad gave me his beloved stallion as a gift when I was thirteen. The horse is rightfully mine, but when Dad died, my mom put her name on Jupiter's paperwork.

As long as she's the rightful owner of him, I need her permission for every event we participate in. It's just another way for her to keep me under her controlling thumb. Her new boyfriend isn't helping matters either.

Turning from my friends, I begin to swim back to the shore. I get no more than ten feet away when my name is called again.

This time it's Callan.

Treading water again, I look at the man I'm growing tired of wasting time on.

"I think my dad is working with that damn eagle again today," he warns from his place on the floating dock. His hand shields his eyes from the high afternoon sun as he squints at me. "It's never done anything, but I don't trust it. Just be careful."

"Oh," I nod once. "Okay."

With that, Callan turns his back on me. Confirming what I already know in my heart and making the disappointment I feel grow.

I don't chase after boys, but our story is the oldest one in the book. A popular upper classman takes interest in the wide-eyed freshman. She's shy but loves that he takes her everywhere, showing her off. He introduces her to everyone like he's truly proud to have her at his side. She believes his whispered sweet nothings and false promises. She becomes swept up in him and thrives off the heat between them.

But what happens when it turns stone cold, and the sweet nothings become lies?

You discover it was all smoke and mirrors, and you're left clinging to something that never existed in the first place.

TWO
ASTOR

JEALOUSY.

It's a peculiar emotion to experience when you're a man who's never wanted for anything. Yet I find that unbecoming shade of green working its way through my system more frequently as of late. It appears during the smallest moments, like now, watching the eagle soar up ahead.

I envy the bird of prey's freedom and ability to fly away from it all. His liberty is fleeting, but every second is priceless to him. I crave those own seconds for myself.

With a low whistle, I call the bird back to me. It's taken years and endless patience to get to this point, but he doesn't hesitate even a moment before swooping back toward the ground. The piece of rabbit leg I have in the leather pouch at my side keeps him coming back.

It's his reward.

Protected by a thick leather glove, he lands gracefully on my arm. He makes a low squawking sound, his yellow ever-observant eyes looking for the treat he knows he's owed.

"Good boy," I praise, stroking a hand down his brown feathers before reattaching the leash to the leather straps around his ankles. It took us a long time to get here, but the contact no longer makes him uneasy. It wasn't an easy road, and I will forever carry scars on my hands and forearms as reminders of our progress.

The outcome has been more than worth it.

Taking his reward from me, he holds the piece of meat in his talons and eats happily as I carry him to the enclosure on the left side of the property. It's built in a dome shape, tight knit black netting covering the whole structure. It's large enough the bird will never feel cooped up, and in the middle is a raised wooden building—almost like a small tree house—where he can escape the Washington rains.

Releasing the tied leash from his foot, I free him, lingering only a moment to watch him fly to a perch. His head nods once, as if he's bidding me farewell as I close the keypad protected door behind me and head back toward my house.

The sound of boisterous laughter and yelling comes from the lake below, reminding me that I'll have another day of college kids in and out of my house. Early in the summer, I made the mistake of allowing Callan to have a few friends over. He has a house on campus he rents with a friend, but they wanted to swim in the lake my house sits on.

Had I known it was going to turn into a weekly event throughout the entire break, I would have rethought my original answer.

Especially had I known he would always bring *her* here.

I've never been one to deny myself what I want, but she is the exception. I've been forced to restrain my cravings for months—something that doesn't come naturally but it is required of me.

It would have been better had she never been put in my sights, but now that I know she exists, I can't seem to escape her.

Now is no different.

I enter through the tall glass backdoors of my home to find

the main source of my growing jealousy standing in my kitchen.

The small triangles of her bikini cover little, revealing her sun-kissed skin. She doesn't hear me enter and her attention remains locked on the phone in her hand.

Even though I know I shouldn't, I take this moment to observe the girl who's unintentionally captured my attention.

She stands on a dish towel in an attempt to not get water on my hardwood floors, but it's not working. Small puddles are forming at her feet. A steady drip comes from her dark hair that doesn't quite reach her shoulders. I watch as a drop falls down her chest. My eyes follow the bead as it travels down her body, stopping only when it disappears into the waistband of her bright yellow bottoms.

The unwelcome desire I feel for the girl rears its ugly head. My teeth clench in anger knowing that, without even trying, she's crawled under my skin. I'm even more infuriated by the fact I've allowed someone so unattainable to do so.

It's one thing to be jealous of another man, it's another thing entirely to be jealous of your own son.

And when I look at Indie Riverton, I'm uncontrollably envious that my son found her first and I'm angry he doesn't fully appreciate the prize he's obtained.

A siren whose song I must ignore.

She's a pretty thing that I'm aching to play with.

A toy that isn't mine to break.

Burying the ill-advised stirrings she causes, I focus on the resentment knowing I can't have her, and I clear my throat harshly.

Her amber eyes drift from the screen and noticeably widen when she finds me standing here. "Mr. Banes," she gasps. "I didn't see you there."

I shift forward a foot, hands behind my back. "You're dripping water on my floors."

She blinks slowly at me as if she's not understanding my

remark. Finally, it clicks, and she quickly says, "*Crap.* I'm so sorry. I needed to check my phone, and I forgot to bring my towel up with me." Keeping her feet planted on the small towel, she reaches for the other dish towel that's folded neatly on the marble countertops. "I'll clean it up," she promises.

Before I can say another word, she squats down and wipes at the puddles on the hardwood. With each one she cleans, another appears from the water still escaping her drenched hair.

Shaking my head, I spin on my heels and head toward the laundry room where I know the housekeeper left a pile of fresh towels.

I return to find her on her hands and knees, a sight that makes my hands flex. Stepping closer, I dangle the towel off my fingertip in front of her face.

Indie's chin lifts, our eyes locking. The prettiest blush I've ever seen spreads across her face as her thin fingers wrap around the offering. "Thank you," she whispers with a sheepish smile.

I don't offer any reply or extend my hand to help her stand. I merely watch the way she nibbles on her bottom lip. It's a nervous tick I've seen her do many times. She does it when she's waiting for Callan to look at her or even acknowledge her. Her big doe-like eyes stare at him, silently pleading for him to remember that she's there, but he never does.

I've never been one to interfere with my son's personal life, and in truth, he's never responded well to hand holding. He needs to make these mistakes so he can learn from them. He'll realize too late that he's fucked up. Though, I'm not convinced his retreat from her hasn't been methodically planned.

"Why are you in here?" I ask. "Shouldn't you be down there with the rest of them?" *With my son.*

Returning to her feet, Indie uses the towel to ring out the moisture from her hair. "I needed a break from the sun." She tells a lie better than most, but the falsehood is written in her amber eyes when she speaks. "And I've been waiting for my mom to get back to me all day about a show jumping event I have this Sunday. She's out of town with her boyfriend, so getting a hold of her has been tricky."

Another thing I've noticed is she also rambles when she's nervous. It shouldn't please me as much as it does that I've caused such a reaction from her. It's not the reaction I desire, but then again, I shouldn't be craving a single thing from her.

"You turned down the spot on our equestrian team along with the scholarship that came with it, did you not?" It was an abuse of my power to look into her school records, but along with my jealousy, my curiosity was also piqued. "Why would you opt for a merit-based scholarship that covers less when you could have received a full ride?"

My question takes Indie by surprise. Her mouth opens and closes a couple of times before she finally finds her words. "I always forget you're the university president and know all this stuff about everyone."

"Not everyone."

Her mouth tilts in a playful smile. "So, I'm pretty special then, huh?"

"No." My correction comes with a terse edge, instantly killing her smile. "When my son is dating a fellow student, I tend to take interest. I'm not fond of having strangers in my home to begin with, and Callan's judgment when it comes to the girls he brings home have been less than ideal."

After his senior year of high school, it went downhill fast and that is partially why I'm shocked he picked someone like Indie.

At the mention of dating Callan, Indie's face falls further, and her hands tighten around the white towel she's still holding. "*Right,* obviously." She nods. "That makes sense."

"Does mentioning my son's past conquests upset you?"

"Upset me? Not at all." Indie makes a scoffing noise before she can help it. It appears it comes as a surprise to even her by the way she covers her mouth. "I... I just mean, I know everyone has a past, and Callan is no different," she attempts to recover, but the damage has been done.

Silence falls between us when I don't offer a reply. Instead, I try to uncover the secrets she keeps guarded behind her pretty face.

She breaks it by answering my earlier question. "I'm good at what I do because of the horse I ride. We're a team, and if I can't compete with him, there's no point in me competing at all. My mom wouldn't allow me to bring him here to Seattle, and without her blessing, my hands were tied. I took the next best option the school offered me, which was the merit scholarship."

"I suppose that makes sense. It takes a long time to establish a bond with an animal, and once they're formed, they're not easily replaced."

Indie glances toward the back yard where I'd just been with the eagle. "I can't begin to imagine the kind of time it took you to bond with him. The patience alone to train an animal like him must have been intense. *How* exactly does one train a golden eagle?"

With her standing this close, I can't help my eyes from wandering across her tanned skin or my lungs from inhaling her. The sunscreen she wears smells of coconut and there's a light trail of freckles on her nose from spending her summer days lounging in my backyard.

"Training something is easy once you know what motivates them, Indie," I begin, my tone sounding darker than I intend it to, but her nearness is destroying my resolve.

Indie picks up on it and her teeth stop their nibbling on her bottom lip. Her eyes lock with mine and her breath shudders as the air suddenly shifts between us. She's looked at me before, but it's as if this is the first time she's truly allowing herself to *see* me.

"For the eagle, it's the promise of food. As long as I continue to reward him, he'll come when I call. Humans are just as easy.

They want money, power, or sex. Once you know which they desire, you can have them eating out of your hand just like the eagle does mine."

She stares up at me with her lips parted and chest rising faster than before. My own heart thuds against my chest and my mind fills with the filthy things I would do to her if she was my plaything.

Indie swallows hard, her throat bobbing. "Which one do you crave?" she boldly asks.

My hand reaches out and I push the wet strand of hair that sticks to her blushing cheek behind her ear. "I don't crave just one, I want all of it," I pause, my hand lingering longer on her skin than it should. "And I'll accept nothing less."

I'm already playing with fire and toeing the line that's been drawn in the sand.

To hell with it.

There are a million reasons to keep my distance, the biggest ones being Indie is Callan's girlfriend and a student at my university, but that doesn't stop me. *Can't* stop me.

Shifting forward another step, I bow my head. I'm not sure if she's even aware that she reacts and moves closer. Her chin tilts up toward me, further bridging the space between us. She's shorter than me by many inches, but we're close enough that I can feel her shaky breath across my chin.

"You would be just as easy," I tell her darkly, eyes cutting to her pink lips. "Once I figured out which reward you craved, I could make you just as obedient. Just like him, you'll come when I call." Even to me, I'm not sure if this is a threat or a promise. Maybe it's a mixture of both. "Just something to keep in mind." Searching for the resolve I originally entered the room with, I harden myself once more. "Please do bring a towel with you next time, Indie. I would hate to see you ruin my floors."

It's best for the both of us that I turn and leave before she can respond.

THREE
INDIE
SEPTEMBER

I WOULD CONSIDER myself a fairly resourceful person.

All my life, I've found a way to achieve my goals and figure out my problems. Sometimes with as little as a piece of bubble gum and spare change at my disposal, I've found a way to *MacGyver* the shit out of life. Each hurdle that's come my way, I've leaped over with grace and my dignity intact.

It took nineteen years, but I think I've finally met my match.

Never in my life have I ever felt more helpless than I do right now. Each direction I look, I can't find an escape route. The doors are all slamming closed on me and I'm hanging on by a single thread.

And she's standing there with a pair of scissors, waiting for the right time to snip it.

I should have seen the betrayal coming, but I foolishly believed that deep down she still cared. She didn't hold back the punches when she proved to me just how wrong I was. Each blow left a bruise that I still wear now. I'm not sure they'll ever fade.

She took the one thing that meant the world to me and now everything else is falling apart in its wake.

It would be easy to blame it all on her, but I'm at fault too. First, for trusting she wouldn't do something so cruel, but for being reckless with my actions in the aftermath. I didn't think through my plan. I allowed the anger and desperation to dictate my moves and now I'm paying the price.

I can only see one way out of this, and there's no chance in hell I'll make it out with my pride intact.

Not when I have to look *him* in the eyes and beg for help.

It's been two months since I even laid eyes on Astor Banes, but that doesn't mean when I close my eyes at night that I don't see him or hear his voice. That singular and brief interaction we had has permanently embedded itself in my brain. I catch myself getting lost in the memory more often than I'd care to admit.

Astor and Callan have many similarities appearance wise with chiseled facial structures and similar builds, but nothing Callan has ever done or said to me has affected me the way his father's words have.

Callan has moments of intensity, but they pale in comparison to the energy that comes off Astor. I felt like I was choking on it that day this summer to the point I couldn't breathe. There are many ways someone can die, but I'm certain at that moment, I wouldn't have minded going out that way.

Prior to that encounter, I was aware of Astor, but never looked at him long enough to get caught in his storm.

Callan has invited me to a handful of family dinners, and Astor was pleasant then. Cordial even. During that time, I was blinded by the whirlwind that was Callan. My rose-colored glasses were firmly in place, and I wasn't seeing past him. Now that the glasses have been lifted and I've finally seen Astor, it's impossible to forget his existence.

He made sure I'd never forget.

"Just something to think about," he'd said, knowing full well what seed he was planting in my head.

The seed has grown into a vine that's been steadily ensnaring me since July. I went out of my way to avoid him, hoping that once he was out of my line of sight, the hold he suddenly had on me would evaporate. I thought it was a fluke, that he'd caught me when I was vulnerable. I was feeling an array of things that day as I was coming to terms with the stagnant state of my relationship with Callan and dealing with my mother.

My walls were down, and I think Astor saw that.

I started to decline Callan's offers to spend time at his father's lake house. It only took two weeks of saying no for him to stop asking all together. At that point, I didn't care because while my boyfriend was floating on an innertube getting drunk in the summer sun, I was busy dodging the shards of my life as they exploded around me. Even if I wanted to go back there and risk coming face to face with the man who's started to haunt my dreams, I didn't have the energy to put on a façade.

And now, after a month of mistakes and fighting battles alone, I'm officially out of options and depleted of all my energy.

I could blame the fact I'm running late to this meeting on being too tired and not wanting to get out of bed today, but it would be a lie. The real reason is it took me two hours of pep talks and psyching myself up to convince myself to go to his office.

By the time I finally did, I only had fifteen minutes to get ready.

It takes effort to not growl in frustration at the hoard of people that slowly exit the elevator. They take their time, like they have nothing else better to do. Meanwhile, I have a meeting with a man who very well might be my last hope of keeping the remainder of my life on course.

If Astor doesn't agree to help me, I'm fucked.

Royally and truly *fucked*.

The last person to exit is a middle-aged woman whose attire

screams *administrative assistant*. She smiles at me as she passes. I usually smile back at everyone, but not today.

Today is not a day for smiles. I feel like I'm on my way to plead with the devil.

I step inside the elevator before anyone else has a chance to join me, my finger holding down the close-door button. Once they're shut, I force a steadying breath into my lungs before selecting the top floor. The ride up is painfully slow, and by the time the doors open, I've carved tiny crescent moons into my palms from digging my nails into them.

This level is quiet—eerily quiet. The phones are silent and there isn't a peep coming from any of the various offices on the floor. Walking down the brightly lit hallway, I start to panic thinking I've selected the wrong floor when a pretty woman with auburn hair stands from the reception desk.

"Miss Riverton?" Her smile is kind, instantly putting me at ease. "Mr. Banes has been expecting you. If you'd please follow me, I can show you to his office."

I feel him before I hear his voice.

"That won't be necessary, Cheska," Astor instructs from somewhere behind me, making chills run down my spine. "I can show her myself."

My muscles feel like blocks of ice, and I'm frozen in place. I don't need to turn around to confirm his slate gray eyes are raking over me. With each pass of them, I can feel them leave trails of fire over my skin.

"Do you need anything else before I leave for lunch?" the receptionist asks, a sultry edge to her voice. I can't say I blame the girl.

"No," Astor tells her, but I know he's still looking at me. "Indie, come with me."

His threat from months ago plays on repeat when I finally turn to face him.

You'll come when I call.

The day in July, he wore dark blue slacks and a white shirt. The first couple buttons had been undone and the sleeves rolled, giving him a relaxed appearance. Today, he's dressed like he's prepared to command a boardroom. Hell, as the president of Olympic Sound University, he might be doing just that after our meeting.

The silver tie he wears complements the silver strands that are forming at his temples and scruff, and the gray color of his suit jacket brings out the slate gray color of his eyes. Both remind me of the color of the sky before a storm rolls in. In all honesty, there's less chaos in a thunderstorm than there is in his eyes. I'd rather face the dangers of lightning than face him.

Not because I'm afraid of him.

No, I'm afraid of what I might do because of him.

Our brief encounter left me feeling unsteady and out of control. He did it so easily, it shouldn't have been possible.

"This way," he instructs, turning away and heading down the hallway. He doesn't turn to make sure I follow. Astor simply knows I will.

It dawns on me as I look around the quiet space that he scheduled this meeting when no is here. And I'm wondering why he'd do such a thing when we enter the spacious office. The whole back wall is made of glass windows, giving an unencumbered view of Puget Sound, one I might find beautiful if I weren't filled to the brim with nervous energy.

Astor takes his seat behind the desk and motions to one of the leather chairs in front of it. My eyes skim over the name plate that sits on the shiny surface.

Astor Z. Banes.

What does the Z stand for?

"Take a seat, Indie."

FOUR
ASTOR

I KNEW the phone call was coming, it just took longer than I expected.

For over a month she's struggled to find a way to fix the mess that has been created and for a month I've waited for her to walk into my office. It would be her last resort, but I knew she would come to me. There was no way she was getting out of this without a helping hand and the public defender that's been assigned her case is worthless. I've met cats that could contribute more than he has. The only decent thing he's done is keep her out of jail.

The last few times I laid eyes on Indie she wore nothing more than a swimsuit. Now she dons a green and black plaid skirt that could be considered too short to some, and a black long-sleeved shirt that's cropped, revealing her toned stomach.

For some reason, I find her attire now more distracting than I did the bikinis. Perhaps it's because I know what's hiding underneath the clothes, or it's more likely because she's wearing black knee-high stockings with her black leather boots. Images of her in nothing but those fill my head.

Indie sits timidly in the chair across from me, her crossed

legs bouncing like she's unable to sit still. The fact that I can make her squirm with hardly any effort pleases me. Fighting a smirk, I cock my head at her.

"What is it that you want from me, Indie?" I know the answer, but I want to hear her say it. I want to watch her pink lips as they form the word, *please*. "You were vague on the phone about what this meeting is pertaining to. It's not about my son, is it?" Asking her this is cruel, but I want to gauge her reaction. Callan hasn't spoken much about her as of late, and I want to know just how fragile the single thread between them is. *How hard will it be for me to break it?*

Her answer won't sway or alter my plans. There's no stopping me at this point, but I would still like to have the information before moving forward.

She shifts in her seat again and her fingers reach up to fiddle with gold necklaces around her throat. "No, Callan doesn't know about this." She pauses, a sad sounding laugh fills the space as Indie shakes her head. "I'm not really sure where we stand and if I did, I still wouldn't want to bother him with it. I'm not sure if he'd care if I did tell him." Amber eyes full of uncertainty collide with mine. "No offense, Mr. Banes, but I have more pressing matters going on than to chase after your son right now."

Even without her saying the words, she tells me exactly what I want to hear.

"Fair enough," I concede, sitting forward in my chair so I can rest my elbows on the black desk. "So, what exactly are you doing sitting in my office right now?"

Indie takes in a lung full of air and slowly releases it before speaking again. "I'm about to lose my scholarship. I've done everything in my power to ensure it's not taken away from me, but like everything else lately, nothing I do is working. The scholarship committee won't even entertain the idea of discussing it further because of what happened."

"And what happened?"

I know the story, but I want to hear it from her.

The uncertainty leaves her eyes and it's replaced with bitter betrayal. "My mother went behind my back and eloped with her boyfriend while they were on vacation. While the ink was still wet on the marriage license, she transferred ownership of our property in Tacoma to Ivan." She's trying her best to keep herself composed, but with each passing second her mask is breaking. "He decided that owning and taking care of such a large piece of land was too much work. He plans on selling everything that sits on it before finally selling the land to a housing developer." Indie's hands ball in her lap, opening and closing. "He also plans on selling Jupiter."

I nod along, allowing her to tell her tale.

"I begged Ivan to let me buy Jupiter from him, but he refused, and my mother wasn't any help. She sat back and let Ivan take him from me."

"While it's a disappointment you won't have the horse in your possession any longer, surely an animal of his skill and caliber will be sold to someone who wants to continue to show him. Correct?"

"No," Indie's head shakes. "They're not doing this to make a profit, they're doing it out of spite."

My head tilts at this remark. "And why would they do that?"

Like she's unable to continue the story from where she sits, she jumps to her feet. She paces behind the chair and her gaze looks anywhere but at me. "A few years ago, there was an...*incident* between Ivan and me. I found a camera in my bedroom that I'd never seen before. I tried to tell my mom about it, to warn her that he wasn't a good man, but she said it was my fault." There's an audible break in her voice when she says the last word. Thoughts of what it'd be like to meet this *Ivan* in person crosses my mind as she continues. "Ivan hated me after that. He's been in my mom's ear ever since, turning her against me. And she's let him." She glances at me for only a minute, like she's making sure I'm still listening. "Ivan won't sell Jupiter for money. He'll sell him to a kill buyer he can find just as a last fuck you to me."

She comes to a stop behind the chair she'd abandoned, her hands gripping the back so tight, her knuckles turn white.

"It's a troublesome story, Indie, but I'm not seeing how any of this affects your scholarship here," I tell her, continuing my ruse that I have no idea what she's done or what she's about to ask of me.

Like I said, I've waited patiently for a month for this meeting. I've been devising and perfecting my plan for her since I learned of the mess she'd entangled herself in.

"I knew who he'd sell Jupiter to and that's why I snuck onto the property while they were asleep. My trainer, Tessa, was a longtime friend of my father's before he passed, and I knew she'd help me. Her friend owns a sanctuary in Idaho, and I thought if I got Jupiter there, he'd be safe." I can practically see the defeat in her bones as her hands drop from the leather chair. "I was so close to the border when the cops Ivan sent found me. They took Jupiter while I was handcuffed on the side of the road and Ivan had me charged with theft of property..."

"And theft is a misdemeanor in the state of Washington," I fill in for her. She doesn't understand it now, but she's lucky she got caught before crossing the state line. Her charges would have been worse had her plan succeeded. "And a misdemeanor on your record disqualifies you for your merit scholarship."

"Yes." Her admission is barely a whisper and is full of defeat.

"And you came here today to ask if I would be willing to pull some strings so you can continue your education here?"

Olympic Sound University is a prestigious private college and the doors that will open for the students once they have their diploma from here are unparalleled. To lose her chance at that on top of everything else that's been taken away from her is unfathomable to Indie. I can practically smell the desperation coming off her.

"Yes."

Some things in life take work and effort, others just fall into your lap like the fates destined it. This is one of those times. I couldn't have planned this better. All the pieces aligned without me so much as having to lift a finger. I promised myself for months, out of respect for Callan, I wouldn't touch Indie Riverton and I would keep my distance from her.

That plan exploded into dust in July when she looked at me with those eyes filled with excitement and fear. A deadly combination but one that sets my blood on fire. The second I left her alone in my kitchen, I decided to break my promise and stop denying myself what I want.

All I had to do was wait for my opportunity and I vowed when it came, I wouldn't hesitate to take it.

She came to me for help but has no idea what it's going to cost her.

Laying my palms flat on the cool surface of my desk, I stand to my feet. Indie's watchful gaze tracks each move I make, like a deer being tracked by a predator. *Pretty girl, I'm going to eat you whole.*

Moving in an unhurried manner, I undo the button of my suit jacket before perching myself on the edge of the desk.

"This is quite the predicament, Miss Riverton." I make a tsking sound. "You made a mess of things, effectively destroying the steadfast path you'd found yourself on." I'm stoking her flames because I want to see how easy it will be for me to put them out again. "It sounds to me that not only have you wasted this university's time, but also its valuable resources. There are thousands of applicants a year for that particular scholarship. They hope and pray to be accepted, but you threw it all away, for what? An easily replaceable *horse*?"

Just like I wanted, fire ignites in her amber orbs and her face contorts in anger. "Don't speak on things that you don't understand," she spits. "You have no idea how important that *horse* is to me. *No idea*. I fucked up, I know I did, but I would do it again if there was a sliver of a chance I could save him from being *slaughtered*." She rounds the chair she'd been using as a shield between us, her fury driving her closer. "As we speak, he could be standing on a scale being weighed so they can determine how much he's worth. They don't give a fuck what his bloodlines are, or how many ribbons he's won. Or even what he means to me. His only value will be in how much meat he can provide and that thought alone is enough for me to throw up on your fucking carpet."

Sitting like a cold piece of stone, completely unbothered by her outburst, I calmly command, "Sit down."

The anger melts from Indie's face, confusion replacing it. She looks between the chair she'd abandoned and me. "*What?*"

"Sit the fuck down, Indie." This time there's a deadly edge to my tone, leaving no room for her to question me.

She stares at me a moment longer before the fight leaves her body once again. Satisfaction fills my chest when she complies with my order without further debate.

So willing to comply, Indie. What else can I make you do?

"Good." My approval has Indie's eyes flaring and ever so slightly shifting in her seat. "You came here for my help, but you haven't said the actual words. So, tell me again, Indie, what do you want from me?"

Her pink tongue swipes out, wetting her bottom lip. Finding the remainder of her plummeting resolve, she tilts her chin and sits up straighter. "Will you please help me, Mr. Banes?"

And there it is. The word I've been waiting to hear.

Please.

FIVE
ASTOR

"YOU REALLY SHOULD HAVE COME to me sooner, Indie. It would have saved yourself a lot of time and energy if you had." I return to the other side of my desk and sit back in the leather chair. Opening the top drawer, I grasp the blue folder that I'd left there nearly two-months prior. Much like me, it waited patiently for this day to arrive. "While you continued with your futile attempts to salvage things, I'd already gone ahead and done so for you."

Indie's lips part in surprise. "I—I don't understand," she stammers.

I place the folder on the shiny surface of my desk. Her eyes flick to it only momentarily before returning to mine. "I knew you'd eventually come to me for assistance, so I took the initiative to pull strings and arrange some options for you in an effort to be well prepared for today." My words come across much more selfless than they are. My motives are and will always be inherently selfish. "It will be up to you which of these two paths you choose, but either way, you will be walking away with a diploma from an esteemed university."

"How could you have known I would come to you? We hardly know each other." Her head shakes.

"Tell me, who else in your life would have been willing or able to help you in anyway?" I question. "Your mother has all but washed her hands of you now that her new husband is in the picture. Your friends could offer you nothing more than a shoulder to cry on. And my son? You elected to not inform him of your troubles. So, I'll ask again, who else was going to help you?"

She sits there, staring at her hands and accepting her fate. "You said I had two options. What are they?"

Opening the blue folder, I push it closer to her so she may read the letter of acceptance from the college in Alabama. "I have a long-time business associate that happens to be the dean of Auburn University. He was more than happy to look past your now blemished record and offer you a place at his school. Housing and a meal plan will also be included as part of your attendance. I have also gone ahead and secured a loan for your tuition. If you should want it, all you would need to do is fill out the remaining paperwork. This would give you the opportunity to start fresh, away from your mother and her new husband."

It's a favorable offer, one that offers her everything she could want. *Almost everything,* that is.

"*Auburn*? Are you kidding me? This offer feels too good to be true. So, what's the catch?"

"Smart girl." My head nods once in approval. Turning over her acceptance letter from the southern university, I reveal the brochure hidden beneath. "They acknowledge talent when they see it and they're not about to let this opportunity pass them by. One of their riders had to leave unexpectedly and there is now a spot on their team available for you."

She stares at the blue and orange pamphlet like it's personally offended her. A reaction I had fully expected. "I already told you that I don't have any interest in being part of an equestrian team. Especially without—"

"Jupiter." I finish for her. She thinks I could have already forgotten the thoroughbred's name. The irony of the name alone will keep it committed to my memory for years to come. "I know what you said, but you're not really in a position to be *picky*, now are you? This offer is one that is not easily beaten. It is also not one you will get again if you were to change your mind in a month's time." Passing the brochure closer to her, I take the picture of the bay-colored horse tucked below it out. "They call him Connecticut. From what I've been told, he's an excellent jumper. He just requires a rider. His owners are alumni of the university and would be proud to have their horse participating on their equestrian team."

Reluctantly, she reaches out with uneasy hands and takes the offered picture. The longer she stares at the gelding in the picture, the more the despair grows in her amber eyes. Her soft lips open and close like she's trying to find the ability to agree to the offer, but in the end her unwavering loyalty wins. Just as I had hoped and planned. Her eyes squeeze closed as she turns the picture over.

Using one finger, she pushes it back to me. "What's option number two?"

There isn't a folder for this one. No, it's best this one isn't written down on paper. "Option two is you stay here, and you're allowed to continue your education here at my university. The same amount that was covered by your scholarship will continue to be covered. Unfortunately, room and board will not be included in this option but seeing as you already have an apartment off campus, nothing will change in that manner. Your classes will resume as normal come Monday morning."

Looking completely dumbfounded, Indie tilts her head at me. "Why didn't you start with that one?"

Leaning back in my chair, I rest my elbows on the armrests

and clasp my hands together. "Because the price for option two is much greater than breaking a vow you've made to yourself."

Her faithfulness to her equine companion is endearing, but I'm about to learn just how resilient it is. If it's as strong as my desire for her, there's a slim chance she will break it.

"To stay at Olympic Sound, what will it cost me?" Indie shifts in her seat, crossing her leg over the other before asking the real question at hand. She's a smart one, I'll give her that. "What do *you* want in return?"

Oh, pretty girl, you have no idea.

That's a deadly question with an answer I'm not sure she's ready to hear in its entirety. So, I tell her the truth. "You."

I watch as she stiffens in her seat and the sweetest airy gasp escapes her lips. "I don't know what that means."

Her hands move to the hem of her short skirt. Her fingers grip the fabric like it's the one lifeline she has left keeping her tethered to her chair. Indie looks like a cornered rabbit, as if any sudden movement will make her flee. I put my theory to the test by standing from my chair once again. Her eyes flick toward the closed door, but like the good girl she is, she remains in her seat.

My palms press flat against my desk as I lean forward, eating up more of the space between us. "It's simple really. For the remainder of the school year, you would be mine. Mine to call upon, mine to have when I please, mine to touch in any way I see fit."

The spark of intrigue that has lingered in Indie's gaze since she walked in my office morphs into dismay. "You want me to, what? Be your *whore*?"

"If you'd prefer to use such degrading terms, we can." *A pretty thing. A pretty whore.*

Her fingers look like they might tear the fabric of her skirt at this point. Her hands have started to shake, but still she remains put. When the door is only mere feet away from her. No one is stopping her from fleeing.

"How can you say that to me when you know I'm Callan's girlfriend?" Indie says this like it's supposed to bring reason to the argument. Little does she know, reason went out the window that day in my kitchen—when I decided I'd no longer deprive myself of what I want.

In steady, unhurried steps, I round my desk and stand in front of her. Indie reclines in her chair, desperately trying to create space between us when I bow so our faces are eye level. She flinches as I trail my fingers along her jaw before clasping her chin in my grasp. I'm forced to hide a smirk when her pupils dilate, and a shaky breath skips across her lips.

"How did that lie taste on your tongue, Indie?" I ask. "Bitter, I'm sure."

She wants to argue with me, I know it, but instead she sits like a piece of stone, allowing the flames to dance just beneath the surface. I know they're there. The flames lick out, teasing me. I want to stoke them.

"So, what's your plan, Mr. Banes?" Her voice is strong, even. "If I said yes to this, you'd turn me over and fuck me right here on this desk? Whether I wanted to or not?"

My smirk finally breaks free. "No, I won't. You have two options in front of you and you must decide which path you'd like to take. If you elect to go to Alabama, I will gladly book you a first-class ticket there and we can end this right here. And separately we can both reminisce over what could have been." No doubt she'll haunt my dreams just as I do hers. "But if you decide to stay and be mine, you must come to me first. If this is the path you decide to take, I will not initiate our arrangement. It ultimately has to be your choice and yours alone."

She tilts her chin higher in my grip. "Why me?"

"You once asked me what I crave. I told you I wanted it all and that included you. Do you remember what else I said that day?"

Her voice is just barely a whisper when she answers, "That you'd accept nothing less."

"*Precisely*. I saw you and decided I wanted to claim you as my own. All I've done now is discovered a way to do so." I don't bother telling her I deprived myself of my craving for months or that I thought of what her pretty face would look like as she looked up at me from her knees. Those are my secrets and mine alone.

She silently ponders this, eyes examining my face like she will find the answers hidden there. I had planned for an array of questions, but she has only one.

"Do I have to decide today?"

"No." I finally release her face from my grasp. "You have until Sunday night. Four days and not a second longer." My fingers pull the card from my suit pocket. It has my personal cell phone number on the back. "If I don't hear from you, I will assume you've found a third path."

She takes the card from me, and I step back, returning to her the space I had been holding hostage. Indie holds the card to her chest as she stands from the chair on shaky legs. Amber eyes look me over once more before she turns from me. It's only when her thin fingers touch the door handle that I speak again.

"I do hope to hear from you, Indie."

SIX
INDIE

SOMETHING WEIRD HAPPENS when someone puts a timer on your life. Seconds you would never think about wasting suddenly feel precious and horribly fleeting.

Three days ago, I left Astor Banes office in a completely bewildered and, frankly, aroused state. The latter, of course, caused an extreme sense of guilt to also bubble to the surface. The idea of being Astor's *whore* shouldn't excite me. The very notion should *infuriate* me and scare me. The rational thing for me to do after leaving our meeting—if you can call it that—was to have run to the closest administrator and filed a complaint against him. Even if I had been inclined to do so, I doubt it would have done anything. Astor Banes is a God among men.

For each second that has passed, thoughts of Astor and his offer have occupied my mind. Not once, not even in my fitful sleep, have I found any reprieve from him. Like my own personal ghost, he haunts me. I can't honestly say I'm mad at him for that. I'm more upset with *myself* that I've even allowed this to be a decision worth agonizing over.

I know which one I should choose. Just like he said, Alabama would offer me a chance at a fresh start, away from the evil doings of my mother and Ivan. I should be asking for the first flight out of Washington. There's nothing tethering me to my home state any longer. My relationship with Callan is nonexistent. At this point, we're both just waiting for the other to call time of death. My mom stopped being my mother when Dad died three years ago and now that she has Ivan, the situation has become even worse. And on top of it all, Jupiter is gone.

Tessa, my trainer, has been calling everyone she knows to try and find where Ivan sold him. Every slaughter and auction lot has been called, but of course they're not willing to give over that kind of information. It's been almost five weeks exactly since Ivan took him and sold him to God knows where. It's starting to feel hopeless at this point. For all I know, he could already be dead.

Not only do I feel like I've let down Jupiter, but I also feel like I've let down my dad. My passion and love for the equestrian world comes from him. His family bred and raced horses in Kentucky for generations. My dad may have ventured away from his family business, but he always had his stables full. His last gift to me before he got too sick was the black thoroughbred. It would crush him today to know the horse he spent years training was gone.

He thought their souls were one in the same and because of that he called Jupiter his heart horse. When cancer became too much and Dad's body could no longer bear to ride, he gave me Jupiter. He knew the horse would be miserable and bored if he were to spend the rest of his long life in a pasture. And when Dad saw how well Jupiter and I worked together, he knew we'd form an unbreakable bond.

My dad's heart may have stopped, but he left a piece of it in his heart horse. That's why the idea of going to Alabama and riding another makes me queasy. To me, it feels like the ultimate betrayal. To *both* of them.

"I have all my connections looking for him, Indie." Tessa's

reassuring tone does little to settle the nerves in my body. "There's a shipment of horses being sent across the northern border in six weeks. Protestors and attempts from different animal-rights organizations—including my own—have set back the original shipment date, but it's looking like they got the go ahead. If we raise enough funds from our donors, Amelia and I are headed there next month to offer to buy the lot. If it works out, there're a few rescues that have offered to help take them in and rehome them once they're rehabilitated. If Jupiter is there, we will find him."

"Okay." I release a long breath, trying to quell the unease that's been a permanent resident in my chest for three days. "Just keep me updated, Tessa."

"We'll get him back. Just hang in there, honey."

"I'm trying." I wish I had a fraction of her optimism right now. "Tell Amy I said hello and thank you." I'm not sure how many lives Tessa and her wife, Amelia, have saved, but I know hundreds of horses would be dead without their endless efforts.

"I will."

The call ends just as Lark's blonde head pops out of the back door I'd escaped from just minutes prior. "There you are. Zadie couldn't find you and we thought you left without saying anything."

Even with her blood alcohol level high and shirt damp from the beer Hansen had spilled on her, Lark has a way of looking effortlessly perfect. She doesn't even try, and the worst part is she's completely oblivious to it. I would hate her if I didn't know she's truly a wonderful person on top of it all.

She's one of the good ones and that's rare here. With a university as prestigious as Olympic Sound comes a lot of money, and with a lot of money comes a lot of corrupt and shady people. There's a select few—particularly a pair of brothers—that I know are in my best interest to avoid. It's best I don't entangle myself in their dark worlds.

"I had to take a call." I wave the phone in my hand at her as I walk up the few steps of the stone patio.

"You and Callan both keep sneaking off with these mystery calls," Lark comments, holding the door open for me. "I feel like I'm always searching for one or the both of you."

The smell of weed and spilled beer suffocate me when I reenter the party. Should I be attending a party when I have less than sixteen hours on my deadline? No, but pacing the walls of my small apartment for a third night in a row felt unbearable. I thought getting out might help me finally make up my mind.

Astor or Alabama?

Or there's always option three where I hold out for a magical third choice to fall on my lap. The option of dropping out of college for now and just working did cross my mind. I could save up enough money to pay for college on my own, but that would take years and completely throw me off track from my plans and goals. I want to be a nurse practitioner, and to do so I will need to get into a master's program. A diploma from Olympic Sound was supposed to be my magic ticket for that. I worked my ass off in high school to make the grades to be accepted here because I knew I'd need a scholarship to afford this school. Even if my mom was, and she's definitely *not*, willing to assist in paying for my education, my dad's illness plundered my family's savings.

I think that's one of the reasons she latched so hard onto Ivan. He has money and isn't afraid to flaunt it. She saw financial security in him.

A red solo cup full of clear liquid is waved in front of me, breaking my train of thought. I take the offered cup from Zadie, who had magically appeared, and look at it with uncertainty.

Reading my unspoken concerns, Zadie reassures me, "Don't worry. I poured it myself." Her bright green eyes are surrounded by her smudged makeup and her red lipstick has long worn off from the various drinks she's had. "Drink up and come dance with me!"

This is why I came here, right? To loosen up and clear my head.

Before I can convince myself to get a cab and go home to stew over my decision more, I toss the liquid back. The vodka burns as it goes down my throat, but I look forward to its impending relaxing affect.

THREE DRINKS later and an hour of dancing, I'm sweaty and just buzzed enough that the dread in my bones has been silenced. Looking at myself in the dirty mirror of the downstairs bathroom, I adjust my short hair. I tie the top half into a messy knot and leave the rest down. All my life I had waist length hair, but when I got to college, I felt like I needed a change. It's progressively gotten shorter, but my current long bob is my favorite look.

"I have to pee!" someone slurs from outside the bathroom before they begin banging on the closed door, alerting me that my time in here is up.

I barely get the door open before a girl dressed in hardly any clothes pushes past me. She doesn't even attempt to close the door before she sits on the toilet and begins to relieve herself.

Shaking my head, I walk down the hallway and search for my friends.

I heard someone yell Callan's name about twenty minutes ago, so I know he's still here somewhere. He hadn't bothered to text me back when I told him I'd be coming to Hansen's party tonight. Lark is right about his constant phone calls. I used to wish he'd tell me what he's working on, but now I don't really care. It's not like I've been forthcoming with my own dealings. Why should I expect him to do the same?

When I showed up at the party, I found him already here, drinking on the back deck with Hansen and their buddies. He gave me a halfhearted side hug that I'd returned with the same enthusiasm, and a kiss on the head. His attention was quickly stolen away by a crude joke from one of the football players. I'd slunk away without a look back.

Looking for familiar faces, I walk into a dark smokey room, and I lock eyes with a pair that are so cold that I feel chills go down my spine. Remember how I said there were people I tried my best to avoid? These cold orbs belong to the youngest brother. He is the embodiment of "if looks could kill," but still I'd rather run into him than his older brother.

My feet skid to a stop and I'm just about to turn away when my eyes zero in on what's actually happening in this dark room.

His tattooed arms rest on the armrest of the chair and his black painted fingernails are digging into the leather. The girl on her knees with her mouth around his dick tries to come up for air, but he doesn't allow it. His lips part in a sneer as his hand leaves the leather armrest to thread through the mussed strands of her hair. He holds her in place and her struggling sounds of desperation fill my ears. She gags as he comes down her throat, and the whole time, I can feel his icy gaze on me.

Where disgust should form in my belly, heat does instead. My lower stomach muscles clench and a tingle runs down my spine. I should be appalled by what I just witnessed, just as I should be appalled by Astor's offer, and yet, the emotion eludes me. It's buried by a hunger and craving I didn't even know I had.

With one last fleeting look at the man hidden in the shadows, I turn away with a fire burning in my belly and an ache between my thighs that *shouldn't* be there.

I search the face of each person I pass trying to find the one who could possibly help ease the growing sensation. I'm at the level of drunkenness where bad ideas are starting to sound like good ones. While the logical side of me knows that Callan doesn't want me any longer and my own emotional ties to him are waning by the second, the physical—*needy*—side of my brain knows that once upon a time, he knew how to please me in ways no one ever has before. Though, the bar was low to start with, but I digress.

But right now, my body wants to relive some of those heated nights.

Hansen stumbles out of a dark doorway up ahead and I push through the small group of students blocking my path to him.

"Hansen!" I shout, getting the tall football player's attention. His head turns around, searching the chaos for the source of the shouting. It's when I pull on the arm of his shirt that he finally sees me. "Hey, have you seen Callan?"

With a huge, *drunken*, smile, Hansen's muscular arm wraps around my shoulder and he pulls me to his side. "Callan is my boy. My boy, man! You know I love him like a brother, but Indie, baby, he doesn't deserve you." His speech might be slurred but his message is clear. "You're too good for him."

I can't stop myself from laughing at this. "Thank you, Hansen." I pat his chest endearingly. "But I don't know if that's true. Actually, I *know* that's not true."

If it were true, I wouldn't be thinking about his *dad*, and I sure as *shit* wouldn't be thinking about the things he could do to my body. I wouldn't lie there at night, envisioning what it'd be like to go to him and allow him to have me in any way he sees fit.

If I were *good*, I would feel shame for wanting to agree to Astor's agreement.

"Nah, don't say that shit," Hansen disagrees. "You're a good one, Indie."

Hansen's words fill my ears, but I'm no longer listening to him. Not really.

For an hour, I didn't think about Astor, but now that I've allowed a single thought of him to reenter my brain, he's consuming me once more. Like a vortex, I'm sucked into my illicit daydreams of Astor Banes and his dark promises.

You would be mine. Mine to call upon, mine to have when I please, mine to touch in any way I see fit.

Hansen cuts through my thoughts, pulling me back. "But to answer your earlier question, Callan dipped out of here about ten minutes ago. I think he was driving Zadie home. That girl thinks she can hold her liquor, but she can't for shit." Someone calls his name across the room, and he pulls away from me. "I'm serious, baby, go find yourself someone better." His grin is huge and encouraging when he looks over his shoulder at me. With a wink, he departs into the crowd.

I stand there, thinking over my next moves. My hand taps a steady rhythm on my bare thigh as I try to talk myself out of what I want to do. *You could learn to enjoy Alabama, Indie. Just take the fresh start and leave everything behind. Leave him and his devious ways behind.*

The thing is, I don't think I'll have to learn how to enjoy Astor. I haven't even tasted him, but somehow, I already know he'll be my favorite flavor.

Before I can convince myself to fly far away from here, I'm pulling the phone out of my small purse and typing in the phone number I'd committed to memory three days ago.

My heart thuds violently against my ribs as the phone rings, and I honestly couldn't tell you if my hands were shaking from nerves or excitement.

He answers on the third ring and the sound of him saying my name makes my breath still in my throat.

"Indie."

"Are you home?" I ask once air fills my lungs once more.

There's a long, heavy pause before he speaks again. "No. I

stopped by my office after a dinner meaning." Only someone like Astor would still be working at this hour. On a *weekend*.

"Will you be there much longer?"

"An hour or so. Why do you ask?"

I'm already walking toward the front door of the house when I tell him, "I'll be there in fifteen minutes."

SEVEN
ASTOR

HER FINGERS TURN the lock on the handle as she rests her back on the door she'd just entered through.

True to her word, it took fifteen minutes for Indie to come to me and I watched each one of those minutes go by on the clock on the wall like a student eagerly waiting for the school day to be done. The knowledge that with each tick of the clock's hand she was drawing closer to being with me—to being mine—made my blood warm and my cock strain against the zipper of my slacks. Never have I waited this long for something, but those months of restraint and patience are about to pay off.

There was a sliver of doubt lingering in my brain while I waited for her to arrive that she wasn't coming here to agree to my offer but instead the Alabama one. But with one look at her flushed cheeks and trembling hands from the adrenaline coursing through her bloodstream, I know my predictions were right. She was always going to come to me and *choose* me.

The black T-shirt style dress she wears is tight, accentuating each one of the curves that hide beneath the fabric. The clunky black ankle boots give her another couple inches of height, something I will appreciate when I have her bent over my desk.

I sit back in my seat and clasp my hands. "Tell me."

Indie wets her bottom lip as she searches for her words. "I want to stay here," she finally manages to say.

"No." My head shakes slowly, making her face fall. "Tell me what I *actually* want to hear."

Not understanding my request, she stares at me with confusion in her pretty features. It would seem I need to better explain myself.

Pushing back in the leather chair, I stand to my full height. As I round the large desk, I begin to undo the sterling silver cuff links in the sleeves of my white button down. I'd abandoned the sports coat in my car when I arrived back at the office after dinner. It hadn't been my original plan to come back here, but with Indie's time allotment running out, I feared I'd go home and stare at the clock. My patience was disappearing faster than her time.

As it was, there were a handful of occasions in the past three days that I drove past her apartment. I had to stop myself from going to her door and demanding her decision right then and there. Just like my other business dealings, I had to respect the deal we had made.

Walking toward her, I drop the cuff links in the pocket of my slacks and begin to slowly roll up the sleeves on my shirt. She stays resting against the door like it's her safety blanket, her chest rising and falling rapidly.

"If you are staying here, you know and fully *understand* what the price is, yes?" I grace her with a quick glance while continuing with my sleeves. "You understand what you'll be if you stay here?"

I come to a stop just inches in front of her, claiming her space as my own. In this position, Indie is forced to tip her head back so she can continue to look at me. Would her eyes still stare at me with such hope and desire if I were to force her onto her knees right here?

"Yes," she breathes. "I understand."

Her nerves and stiff posture soften when I caress her face with my fingers. Her eyes flutter closed with contentment, thick lashes brushing against her cheekbones, but the sweet moment is ripped away when I harshly thread my fingers through the short strands of her hair. Amber eyes clash with mine once more and a startled gasp escapes her lips as I force her head back even farther.

Dipping my head, I bite out between clenched teeth, "Then say it."

I expect to find a flicker of apprehension reflected on her face, but to my utter delight, there isn't a single trace.

She's ready.

"I want to be yours."

Her declaration has chills of pleasure snaking down my spine and limbs before convening at my cock. It presses against my zipper, aching for her. I should take her right here up against this door, but for just a little while longer, I will have to gather my remaining control.

"Prove it. Show me that you want me."

I pull harder on the strands of her hair, and she hisses out a breath. "How?"

"Touch yourself," I demand, releasing her and stepping away from her. "Touch your cunt and show me how wet you can get without me laying a single finger on you."

Her teeth sink into her bottom lip while a beautiful blush rises on her cheekbones. "I don't…"

"Don't *what*? Want to?" I offer as a possible answer as I slowly stalk backward to my desk. If she's already refusing me this early on, I may have a lot more work cut out for me than I originally thought. "Or perhaps, it's that you don't know how?" Perching on the edge of my desk, I wait for an answer.

Like she's trying to hide her growing, and obvious, blush, she stares at the carpet when she speaks. "I know how—*of course,* I know how. It's just *private*. I just don't do it in front of... *people.*"

My eyes narrow in suspicion. "You've never fingered yourself while your lover watched?" More importantly, none of her past lovers have bothered to ask her to? What an oversight on their part.

A small head shake is the only reply I get.

"Look at me." My order has her head snapping up like someone has struck her. "Let's get something straight, Indie. For the duration of our arrangement, your private moments are no longer your own. They now belong to me, just as you do. Your body, your orgasms, and your fucking *tears* are mine. As are the remainder of your firsts. I'm going to take each one of them and claim them as my own. You say you've never finger fucked yourself in front of a lover? Come here and let me be the first to witness such a sight."

Her face is full of apprehension, but I can see the spark in her eyes. Indie can deny it, but my order thrills her. "Okay," she agrees after a steadying breath.

"Good girl." I praise. "Stand in front of me."

Her footsteps are slow and measured as she walks toward me. Just like she did when she was before me last, her fingers fiddle with the thin gold chain around her throat. Once she's a foot in front of me, my hand lifts and she comes to a stop.

My eyes start at her boots and trail up her bare legs. "Are you wearing panties?"

"Yes."

"Take them off."

Indie hesitates only a second before her fingers trail up her thighs. My teeth grind as her hips subtly sway while she pulls the scrap of black lace from her body. The fabric falls to her ankles and one leg at a time, she steps out of them. Boldly, she locks eyes with me and bends at the waist to scoop them up.

Standing back to her full height, she dangles the thong from her fingertip. A move that reminds me of when I gave her the towel in July.

"Give them to me."

I take the offered trophy from her finger and immediately bring them to my face. Her eyes widen as I take a greedy inhale of the fabric. "You're going to smell even better when you're completely dripping with need for me." There's already a dampness in the fabric, but I want to see just how wet she already is. My head nods at the chair a foot in front of me. It's the very one she'd sat in just days ago. "Sit down."

Gingerly, she sits down with her hands in her lap and her legs closed tight together. The dress she wears hikes up another inch, but not enough for me to see what I crave. She's so close, I could reach out and touch her myself, but I want to see her do it first. I want to see just how much power I have over my good girl.

"Are you going to deprive me of what I want, Indie?" My voice comes out with a harsh bite. A clear warning to her.

She swallows hard. "No, I'm not."

Inch by inch, her legs slowly open for me until I'm rewarded with the sweet sight of her pretty pussy, but at this angle it's still not enough for me. It's obscured and I want to see it all.

Reaching down, my hands wrap around her calves. Indie's gasp echoes through the room when I plant her booted feet on either side of me on the desk—effectively caging myself between her legs. This position change forces her to slide lower on the leather chair and spread her legs wider. Like a beast, a hum of satisfaction comes from my throat when it gives me the exact view I want.

Every piece of her is on display for me.

"Show me how you come on your own fingers."

EIGHT
INDIE

NEVER IN MY life have I felt more self-conscious and turned on than I do with my feet on the desk, spread eagle with Astor between my legs. There's no hiding from him, no angles that I can turn to spare myself from some of the embarrassment I'm experiencing. I'm completely bared to him.

It's an odd thing to be riding the line between excitement and fear, but if I'm going to be Astor's, it's a place I'm going to have to get comfortable being. Somehow the fear makes it all even more intense.

Astor's gray eyes stare at my pussy like he's seeing his long-awaited prize. And it only furthers the heat forming in my core and makes my need for him grow.

This isn't the first time I've used my fingers to get off, and it's not the first time I'll do it thinking about Astor Banes either. But it's the first time I've ever touched myself while someone watched. I don't know why it never occurred to me that doing something like this in front of a partner could be exhilarating, but the second he told me that's what he wanted, anticipation shot through me.

Starting from the gold charm around my neck, I drag my

fingers downward. While I'm thrilled to get the chance to ease the ache between my legs, I'm more intrigued by the way Astor's eyes narrow and his nostril flare when my fingertips trace along the seam of my pussy. Somehow, pleasing him feels more important than pleasing myself.

Air rushes through my parted lips when I make a slow, teasing circle around my clit. I'm not sure if I'm taunting myself or Astor, but I do it again, slower this time. The only tell it affects Astor is the way his hands tighten around the edge of the desk and his knuckles turn white.

Repeating myself, I add pressure this time and my hips flex instinctually upward. When I masturbate at home, under the protection of my sheets, it takes a lot of patience for my body to become receptive to my own fingers. I can get there, but it usually takes me more time than I'm willing to give. My pink vibrator gets the job done a lot faster.

But under Astor's watchful gaze, my body is responding faster than it ever has. It makes me wonder what it is about him that is so different from the others. At one point, I thought there was unmeasurable chemistry between Callan and I but knowing how Astor can make me feel with just a single look, I know the heat I thought I once had would be tepid in comparison.

My fingers travel lower and tease my opening. I know what I'll find when I sink them inside. Astor said he wanted to make me wet without touching me but when I pressed against that door with his hand threaded in my hair, my body was already reacting to him.

"That's it," Astor encourages as I push one digit inside. "Get yourself so wet that you're dripping for me when I finally touch you. I want you ready to take my cock."

"I'm ready," I moan, adding another finger. It quickly becomes coated just like the other one. "I want you now."

"Begging for me already?" His taunt only adds to the pulsing in my pussy and making my nipples tighten. "Give me what I want first, then I'll do the same for you. Keep going, pretty girl."

Pretty girl.

The name sends me reeling. My fingers move faster, thrusting as deep as I can manage myself. I know that if he were the one touching me, he would be able to reach all those sensitive places hidden inside of me. My eyes glance at his large hands still wrapped around the desk like he's holding himself back. Fuck, I bet he could reach places I didn't even know existed.

And that's why when I drag my fingers out of my drenched pussy and begin to circle my clit with them once more, I imagine it's him sending shocks of pleasure through me. That it's his callused hands making my core muscles quiver.

A sharp jolt of ecstasy has my legs closing and my feet lifting off the desk as they pull back toward me. Astor's hands lock around my ankles and force my legs back open. He places my feet back on the desk and instead of letting me go again, they remain in place, keeping in the position he wants.

The idea of being restrained has always intrigued me, but I've never felt ballsy enough to admit that to any of my past boyfriends. I get the feeling that it won't have to be a discussion I have with Astor. It will simply happen.

My pace quickens and my movements become erratic, gone are the slow teasing circles from before. The orgasm I've been chasing is so close, I can feel the hum building under my skin.

All I need is one little push, and I'll be sent over the edge.

And Astor knows this. "I want to know if the sounds you make are as sweet as the rest of you." His words wash over me like a liquid fire. "Come for me."

My orgasm bursts through me, and I lose all control of my body. I can't breathe as I writhe in the chair, riding wave after wave of pleasure while my fingers continue to strum my clit. My legs try to close involuntarily again, but Astor's vise-like grip keeps me in place and forces me open so he can watch as my pussy pulses with each chaotic wave.

His hands fall away once I regain control of my body. My vision clears and I find his gray eyes licking over me like a starved man who's just been served dinner.

"Beautiful," Astor praises darkly. "Just like I pictured it—better even."

The fact that he's pictured such a thing sends another flood of heat through my veins. Were we imagining such a moment at the same time? While I lay in bed thinking of what it'd be like to cross the line with him, was he imagining me spread out before him?

He leans forward and looms over me. I've been close enough this whole time that he could've touch me if he so wished, but that's not what he wanted. That moment has passed, and I know from the hungry look in his eyes that he's grown tired of being just an observer.

Starting at my ankles, Astor's fingertips trail up the inside of my legs. Goosebumps follow in their wake and shivers shoot across my skin. I expect him to reach for my pussy, to touch me like I hope, but he doesn't. He clamps his fingers around my hand that still rests on my lower stomach.

"Tell me, Indie, while you touched yourself, who consumed your thoughts? Who did you think about while you came? Callan, perhaps?" His question has my head snapping up and eyes flaring. The smirk on his face lets me know that my reaction pleases him. "Or did you think of me? Did you imagine it was my hands worshiping your cunt?"

I swallow hard, finding the ability to speak again. To speak the complete and utter truth. "I thought of you. I have since July."

I'm forced to drop my feet back to the floor when Astor's hand tightens around my wrist, and he pulls me back into a sitting position. He examines my glistening fingers and brings them to his mouth. Even if I wanted to, I couldn't pull my hand away from him. His grip is unwavering—borderline painful.

My mouth waters watching as he sucks my fingers clean. His eyes lock with mine and the dark look that's reflected in them makes me choke on my breath. With each pass of his tongue on my fingertips, the flame he ignited in my core grows hotter.

Removing my fingers from his mouth, Astor's features twist with arrogance. "I can taste your honesty." With a harsh yank, he forces me back to my feet. I sway for a second, uneasy on my feet. "And it's fucking delicious."

Everything happens so fast. One second, I'm standing in front of him and the next I'm bent over the desk that he'd just seconds ago been sitting on. Standing behind me, Astor's hand trails between my thighs before delving into my wet center. His hiss of approval fills me with a sense of pride.

"My pretty girl does just what she's asked," he praises, the tip of two of his fingers running along my opening. "You're dripping for me, Indie."

"*Yes.*"

The sound of a zipper has my head turning and cheek pressing into the cool surface of the desk. Anticipation pools in my stomach like lava and my knees already feel weak at the thought of what's to come.

"I've waited too long for this," is the only warning I get before the thick head of his cock is shoved into me.

NINE
ASTOR

I THOUGHT I WAS PREPARED, that I'd envisioned this in my head enough times that I knew what it'd be like to finally have her, but I was wrong. Nothing could have prepared me for how it feels to be fully seated inside her pulsing pussy. I'm not sure if it's the triumph I feel knowing that my waiting is over and she is finally mine, or if it's simply just *her*. That she is this sweet and tight, it wouldn't have mattered if I had to wait or work for her, Indie still would have felt like a dose of pure ecstasy straight to my veins.

It's something I will never know for sure, and in this moment, I can't find a single fuck to give. Not when her pussy is clamping down on me like it is, and her beautiful noises are filling my ears.

The guilt for taking her right from under my son's nose has always been scarce, but it's completely nonexistent now. Now that I know what it's like to have her as my own, the emotion eludes me entirely. Something that feels as good as Indie shouldn't cause guilt.

I pull almost completely out of her before plunging back into her slick heat. I pull a ragged moan from her. The sound vibrates off the floor to ceiling glass windows. It's too late for people to be at the office, but the chances of the cleaning crew lingering about is high.

My last name carries an unmatched level of protection. Even still, if word were to get out about my dealings with Indie, there would be whispers, but no one is stupid enough to do it in my presence or on my campus. The people in my social groups wouldn't dare try ruin my reputation because they know they'd never win. If they became too bold and truly attempted it, it would take one call to my family on the east coast, and they'd be taken care of quietly and efficiently. And the best part? My hands remain perfectly clean of blood, like they have for years.

Like Indie, I hadn't even bothered to remove my own clothing. My pants are pushed down just enough to free my erection. My hand releases her hip to pull the thong I'd confiscated from her out of my pants pocket.

My other hand threads through her hair and I yank her head back toward me, forcing her back to arch at an aggressive angle. Wide eyes collide with mine as I stuff the lace into her mouth.

"Don't spit these out," I order. "Be a good girl and keep quiet. We can't have anyone hearing you."

Her protest is cut off when I thrust into her again in a long deep stroke. Her groans come out strangled and muffled, just the way I need them to be.

"I'm going to take you so fast and hard you will still feel me inside of you for days. Every time you move, you're going to be reminded of what I did to you. That I've stolen you and claimed you as my own." There are some lines that aren't meant to be crossed, stealing another man's woman is one of them. I saw that line and set it on fire. Rejoicing as it burned.

Releasing her hip from my punishing grasp, I lift one of her legs off the ground and up onto the desk. Her nails dig into the surface, and I wonder if I will find scratch marks in the wood finish tomorrow. For some reason, the thought of her leaving her mark on my property thrills me. It's evidence that she was there.

I thrash into her, not letting up or slowing down. This isn't for her. It's for me. She's already come once tonight, and if she comes again now, it'll be an added bonus for her, but it's not my priority. Not when I'm trying to leave my mark on both her skin and soul.

I may not be the first man to fuck her, but I am going make it so that all her past lovers become dull memories, and her future lovers become inadequate. Each man she fucks after me will pale in comparison to me and what I've done to her body. Never will she forget me, and that's another way I will leave my mark on her.

When our arrangement has long passed, she will still think of me. I will own her memories.

I'll push her to her limit, taking everything she's willing to give, and stealing what she's not. Her pussy walls clamp around me with each violent thrust and her hips move, matching my rhythm. She doesn't beg me to stop around her gag or push me away. She eagerly takes it and thanks me with her chorus of moans.

My eyes watch as my cock disappears in and out of her soaked pussy. It's a sight that will be seared into my brain for all my years to come. One I will savor on my deathbed.

The tight ring of muscle catches my attention and wicked ideas fill my mind. "Has any man ever had you here?" I question darkly as my thumb presses against her asshole on my next thrust. Instantly, her body stiffens and her head snaps in my direction. The look of pure fear in her eyes gives me my answer. "I look forward to being your first." I continue to add pressure with my thumb, but don't push inside. Yet. "We'll work on getting your ass ready to take my thick cock soon, Indie."

There might be apprehension in her eyes, but the heavy moan

that comes from her gagged mouth and the tightening of her pussy around my dick lets me know the idea excites her.

I'm getting close and my fingers dig into her hips, no doubt leaving marks in her sun-tanned skin. My teeth grind as I try to keep my release at bay so I can stay in her warm cunt as long as possible, but I can't hold it off any longer. Based on the flutter building in her walls and the cries she's making, Indie is just as close.

Pulling out of her, I flip her violently onto her back. I'm too far gone that I can't tell if the cry she makes is from pain or pleasure. Fisting my cock, I stroke it twice more before I come all over her bare pussy. Indie groans, throwing her head back and I bite out a harsh curse at the sight.

Using one hand to keep her legs spread wide for me, I spread my cum through her soaked and swollen pussy. She jolts when I brush over her clit. She's still close, her orgasm just a hair's breadth away.

"I could get you off with one touch right now, couldn't I?" I pant, still out of breath. "Should I reward you for being so good?"

Big amber eyes silently plead with me as her head nods desperately.

I could deprive her, but instead I decide to please her. "Okay, pretty girl. Fall apart for me."

And she does.

TEN
ASTOR

SHE'S TRYING to get her ass spanked until it blisters, I swear.

One week into our arrangement and she's already ignoring my messages. That was part of our deal, that she would come when I called, but for five hours now, she's failed to respond or show up at my door like the good little girl I know she can be.

Instead of paying attention to the board meeting like I should have been, I stared at my dark phone screen, and silently became more enraged. Exiting the meeting as abruptly as I did had many confused looks being shot in my direction, but I couldn't stand to sit there when Indie is already defying me. We agreed she would be at my beck and call for eight months. Not eight days.

My hand grips the leather steering wheel tighter as I accelerate around a minivan driving too slow for my liking. The engine of my Porsche Cayenne is the only sound to occupy the short drive to her apartment. I'm too angry to listen to the radio.

My tires squeal when I turn down the one-way street she lives on. From the research I'd done on her, I know exactly which windows belong to her studio apartment. While I approved of her being smart and keeping her white curtains pulled tight, I frequently found myself disappointed I couldn't get a glimpse of her.

But it's not the windows that draw my attention this time, it's the yellow moving truck parked in front of the building and a forlorn looking Indie standing on the sidewalk, watching as pieces of furniture are hauled into the vehicle.

A mover wearing a T-shirt the same color as the moving truck walks past her with a woven basket of various things. Indie shouts something at him and jumps in front of him to stop him from walking off. The man's face pulls with irritation and yells back at her. She tries to reach for the basket, but he snatches it away from her.

When she tries again and this time he pushes her back, my foot slams on the brakes. I'm throwing the car into park and abandoning my vehicle in the middle of the street before Indie even has a chance to react to being pushed.

Stalking up behind the pair, I call her name, "Indie!" It comes out in a harsh snap, my annoyance with her blatantly ignoring me still evident in my tone. Heads turn in my direction and wary eyes scan me. Indie glances over her shoulder briefly in a distracted manner, but instantly does a double take when she finds me walking in her direction.

Her lips mouth "*fuck*" before turning back around to face the man with the basket.

That's right, pretty girl, you're in trouble.

Hands clasped behind my back, I come to a stop next to her and look between the dueling pair. "What's going on here?"

"Nothing," the mover snaps. "She's just getting in the way of the job we were *hired* to do."

"You have no right to take this," Indie's hands grab for the basket full of what looks to be various personal items like picture frames, a jewelry box, and pieces of random clothing. "Everything in front of the fireplace is mine to keep. That was the deal she made. This basket was part of that pile."

"I took this out of the bedroom," he argues, not backing down. "It goes with the rest."

"Why are you lying?" Indie's hands thread through her messy hair. It looks like she may have fallen asleep with wet hair. Scanning the rest of her, I find she's still wearing her pajamas and slippers. The thin cotton shorts do very little to conceal her ass. She's dressed like she's been resting all day but the dark circles under her eyes make me think she hasn't slept at all.

Not liking that I haven't been given an answer yet, I hold her chin in my fingers and force her head to turn in my direction. The mover takes the opportunity to slink away.

Indie stares up at me, the same defeat that shone in her eyes when she first came to me for help resides there again. "What are you doing here?" she asks instead of answering my silent question.

My grip tightens on her face. "Really? That's all you have to say to me?" The realization she's made a mistake is immediate. Her mouth opens to speak again, but I cut her off. "You ignore my messages all day—a strike against our agreement—and then force me to come and *search* you out? I don't come to you, Indie. You come to me." I glance at the jackass in the ugly yellow shirt loading the basket into the truck. "And when I do find you, another man is putting his hands on you? Have I not made it abundantly clear that I'm the only one who gets to touch you?"

"Are you kidding me? It's not like I asked him to touch me."

"It happened nonetheless," I snap. "I don't repeat myself, Indie, but this one time I will. What is happening here?"

Her eyes squeeze closed like she's fighting tears. "Another gift from my mother and Ivan." She tries to turn her head away from me and I reluctantly allow it. "I keep thinking she couldn't stoop any lower, but she keeps proving me wrong. I never thought she'd make me homeless."

"I thought you paid for your housing yourself?"

"I did—I *do*! The private lessons I teach for young riders a couple times a week pay for the apartment, but it's *Mom's* name on the lease. I couldn't qualify for the apartment on my own because I didn't have any credit to my name. Mom never allowed me to get a credit card or even pay for my own phone bill. It wasn't until I turned eighteen that I got those things, but by then, she'd already put her name on the dotted line. It never occurred to me when I accepted her offer to sign for the apartment that she'd use it against me. I thought she was doing it to be helpful and kind like she used to be before Dad died. Which I now know was foolish of me."

My eyes narrow. "You really believed the woman who allowed you to be charged with *theft* would allow you to stay in an apartment with her name on it? Surely, you can't be that naïve."

"I'm sorry for holding out hope that she would still be my *mother* and *care* about me. It's a mistake I won't make again."

"Good."

It would be hypocritical of me to criticize Indie's mother seeing as I'm by no means the picture of a perfect parent. Far from it, but the more that comes to light about her and the new husband, the more I believe the world would be a better place without them in it. Indie's life, without a doubt, will be exponentially improved without them being permanent fixtures.

"Did she pay the fine to break the lease?"

Indie nods. "Yeah. Showed up at my door at six this morning and told me I had an hour before the movers showed up. Told me I could keep as much as I could pack in that time, the rest was to be taken for donation or the landfill."

Two movers carrying a cheap looking loveseat walk past us to the truck. Indie watches helplessly as her belongings are taken one by one from her. "Where do you plan on staying in the meantime?" There's a long waitlist for a place in the dorms on campus and unless her credit score has improved in the short time she's had building it, I doubt she could qualify for another apartment so quickly.

With an exhausted sigh, Indie rubs her face. She looks like she needs a shower and a good night's sleep. "Lark offered me her couch for the time being. It's a small studio apartment, but it's better than paying for a hotel room every night. We'll make it work."

This new living arrangement won't work for me at all. "How are we supposed to keep our dealings a secret when you're living with a fellow student? Your constant sneaking off will become noticeable, and one accidental slip of the tongue to her could ruin it all." Another pair of men carrying out an entertainment center forces us to step off to the side of the walkway. "Your body is supposed to be at my constant disposal. You should be rested and ready for me at any given time. That won't happen if you're sleeping on some college student's fucking couch."

"I don't have any other options right now. Until my credit score is higher, and I've saved up enough money from my lessons for first and last month's rent, I can't get my own place. I apologize if that puts a *kink* in your plans for me, Mr. Banes," she snarls my name like a curse.

I step into her and sneer close to her face. "Watch your fucking tone and remember who the fuck you're talking to, Indie."

The fight instantly melts from her body and her eyes fall to the slippers on her feet. "Yes, sir."

Finding her response more than satisfactory, I retreat a step and watch the commotion around me. Solutions and options circulate in my brain, but there's only one that's truly acceptable to me. "Go collect whatever remains of your belongings," I order.

"What?" She frowns. "Why?"

"You're coming home with me."

"Why would you want that? That's not part of our deal."

It never occurred to me to have her live with me for the duration of our arrangement, but now I am wondering why I hadn't thought of it before. It's brilliant really. "But you're wrong. This plays perfectly into our deal. What better way to have quick access to you and your sweet body than to have you sleeping right down the hall from me? This way I don't have to wait for you to come to me. I can simply start every morning with you as breakfast and fall asleep with the smell of your pussy on my skin."

My words cause a flush to form on her cheeks. "This doesn't feel like a good idea. What about Callan? What we're doing—what we've done already—is *wrong*. We're not officially broken up and that's bad enough, but now you want me to move into his *home*?"

If she knew the full truth when it comes to her situation with Callan, she wouldn't be experiencing any doubt or shame over the game we're currently playing together. That's a clarity that I can't offer her; it's something my son must set right himself.

"When was the last time you had a real conversation with Callan? Not one over text, but face to face? Let me rephrase that, when was the last time you actually laid eyes on Callan?"

Her teeth bite into her bottom lip. "It's been a week or so," Indie's admission is low, just barely a whisper.

"And yet you are standing here trying to tell me that you're still together." My head shakes at her.

"It's the *principle* of it. There needs to be a clear end to our relationship, not this weird uncommunicative drift-apart thing we're doing. We need to say the words face to face, not over text. I've tried, but he keeps ignoring my messages about meeting somewhere," she sighs in frustration. "And when it finally happens, it's going to be even weirder to be living in my *ex*-boyfriend's home."

"It's *my* home," I correct. "And I'll deal with my son. Now, go get your things, Indie."

ELEVEN
INDIE

FOR MONTHS, I avoided Astor and his lake house, and now here I am, hanging my clothes up in the guestroom walk-in closet. The guest room that is right down the hall from Astor's bedroom.

If someone had told me back in July that not only would I be living with Astor Banes, but also fucking him like he's the only thing that can provide me with oxygen, I would have laughed my ass off. Even now, it feels surreal. I keep waiting for someone to pinch me and wake me up from the fever dream my life has become.

With my clothes neatly packed away, I begin pushing the handful of boxes and baskets I'd had time to pack across the room. There isn't any reason to unpack those as well. It's my plan to be out of Astor's home as soon as possible. I need my own space I can escape to after he's finished afflicting my body with his devious ways. A place where I can collect my thoughts away from his intense gaze.

He was right that night in his office. I was going to feel him for days after he'd ruthlessly taken me on his desk. Two days later, when he summoned me back, my pussy was still sore. To my utter surprise, the zing of pain when he fucked me again ended up increasing my pleasure.

I'd expected to discover new things about myself during my time with Astor, but I wasn't prepared for them to be revealed so fast. Things I never knew I wanted are being taught to me daily.

And each day I wake up eager to learn what's next.

Pushing the last cardboard box into the closet, I turn to grab the container I had filled with the ribbons Jupiter and I won together. They'd been the second thing I'd packed, right after the basket with my pictures. My already broken heart cracked more when the mover refused to give the basket back to me.

I should have been better prepared for my mom and Ivan's next moves. Astor is right, taking the apartment from me was an obvious choice for them. I don't know why I continue to naïvely believe that my mom will one day return to the woman who raised me. There's no way that she's always been this cruel and bitter. I remember walking the pasture with her and picking wildflowers in the summer, and I remember decorating cookies in the kitchen. My dad had taken a picture of us with blue frosting coating our teeth. The very picture was one of the ones in the basket from earlier.

Where is that mom? Where is the woman who read me bedtime stories?

I think she died when my dad did because I don't recognize the vile woman she's become in the past three years.

Blowing the hair that's fallen from my short ponytail out of my eyes, I reach down for the basket of ribbons but stop short when I spot something sitting just inside the door of the room. I'm not sure when it was placed there, but it makes an embarrassingly large smile grow on my lips.

The basket with my pictures and grandma's old jewelry box is *here*.

How? I watched him load it into the moving truck.

Surely Astor wouldn't have retrieved it for me. That would

be wildly out of character for him and borderline unbelievable. *Right?*

Walking to the open doorway, I look down the hallway for signs of him, but it's quiet with zero sign of movement. Or Astor.

He'd disappeared after helping me carry the boxes inside, saying he'd give me time to settle in. As if I could ever really settle in here. I feel ridiculously out of place. Everything is neat and pristine, not a single sign of clutter anywhere. I'm almost afraid to touch anything.

Stashing the magically appearing basket in the closet with the rest of my belongings, I disappear into the attached bathroom that's made completely of white marble and gold fixtures. I'll search for Astor after I've had a chance to wash this horrible day off me.

I SHIELD my eyes from the late afternoon sun, watching as the golden eagle cuts through the sky with an elegance that's hard to put into words. The animal is magnificent on its own but watching how it works with Astor is a sight to behold. They make it look effortless where I know it's anything but. It's evident in the way they respond to each other that years of patience and trust went into this relationship.

Astor releases a long, low whistle and the bird of prey swoops back down to where Astor waits. The animal is an alarming size, but Astor doesn't bat an eye when it lands on his gloved arm. The wingspan has to be over six feet long and I can see the wicked sharp talons from where I stand on the deck above them.

He hasn't noticed me observing them, but I prefer it that way. I want to watch him like this for as long as I can.

There's always a swirling storm circulating around Astor. His energy is turbulent and untamed, but I've never seen him calmer that he is now, working with his eagle. It's the same kind of peace I found while working with Jupiter.

He pulls out a hunk of raw meat from the leather pouch on his hip and walks across the yard toward the enclosure located on the other side of the property. Say what you want about Astor Banes, but he truly cares about that animal. The expensive state-of-the-art aviary he had custom built proves that.

I'm sitting in one of the patio chairs checking my phone for any updates from Tessa when Astor returns to the house ten minutes later. He doesn't say anything, just leans against the deck railing and stares at me. His gray eyes lick over my skin, causing liquid heat to spread through my body.

"Your whistle command reminds me of something my dad used to do," I start, needing to break the silence. "He trained all his horses to respond to a certain whistle. It always reminded me of a bird's call. He'd stand at the pasture gate and do it. No matter how far they were, the horses always heard him and came running. When he became too sick to ride and gave me Jupiter, I would use the same whistle every time I entered the barn. Jupiter would always whinny back from his stall. It's like it became our way of greeting each other. It became a habit I guess because I still do it every time I enter the barn I teach my lessons at. I know Jupiter is gone, but a small part of me still expects him to answer."

Astor doesn't offer any kind of response to my story other than a small nod of his head. It's the only proof I have that he'd even heard me speak.

Putting my phone down on the small side table, I sit up straighter in my seat and clear my throat. "Does he have a name?" My head nods in the direction of the eagle's enclosure.

"He does."

My lips twitch at his very on-brand answer. "Are you going to tell me what it is?"

The fabric of his black button down pulls tight around his shoulders when he crosses his arms in front of him. He might be twenty or more years older than them, but Astor is in better shape than most of the college students I know. I haven't had the pleasure of seeing him without a shirt, but I would bet money that there's a nice set of abs hiding under there.

"What will you give me in return?"

He wants me to walk into the trap he's just cleverly laid, but unfortunately for him, I'm a quick learner.

Uncrossing my legs, I stand up from the wooden chair. "That's a trick question, Mr. Banes. You and I both know that I don't have to *give* you anything because it's already yours to take. That was the deal, was it not?" A smirk spreads across my lips.

The approval in his eyes makes the muscles in my lower stomach tighten. "Good answer."

"I thought so." I stop in front of him, just far enough that he can't reach me.

Astor's eyes lock on where my fingers play with the short hem of the flowy sundress I'd thrown on after my shower. He doesn't look up when he answers. "His name is Periphas. In the legends, Periphas was a mortal king whose following's adoration began to rival Zeus's. Out of anger and jealousy, Zeus had the king turned into a giant golden eagle. Periphas then became the mighty God's personal messenger and companion."

"I didn't know you were into Greek mythology."

"I'm not," he corrects instantly. "My mother was. She lived in Greece in her youth and would tell my brothers and me the myths as bedtime stories. The one of Zeus and his eagle always stuck with me and when I got my license to own a golden eagle myself, the name seemed fitting."

Astor sharing personal details of his life feels like something that doesn't come naturally to him, but I appreciate him telling me the story nonetheless. Makes me understand him just a small amount more.

He holds his hand out to me. "Come here." It's not a request, it's an order. Releasing the hem of my dress, I place my hand in his much larger one. He pulls me forward by it before placing it on the railing of the deck. "Put your other hand up there too and don't fucking move them."

The shift in his tone and demeanor is abrupt, but my body is happy to go along with it.

Stepping behind me he begins to trail his fingers down either side of my body. He starts at my bare shoulders and slowly travels down to the hem of my dress I'd been fiddling with just moments before.

"I want you to wear this dress tomorrow at dinner," he rasps close to my ear as his hands push the fabric up. He hums in approval when he finds I'm wearing nothing under my dress.

Confused by what dinner he's talking about, I try to turn around to face him. The second my fingers lift off the railing, his palm comes down on my ass in a harsh smack. "What did I tell you?"

Startled and confused by my body's reaction to his strike, it takes me a second to fully comprehend his question. Swallowing, I say, "Don't move my hands."

"*Precisely*," he murmurs. "Bend forward and spread your legs, pretty girl. I want to see my cunt."

His.

Every piece of me is *his*.

I do what he says, exposing myself to him. "What dinner are you talking about?" I whisper, hands flexing on the railing.

My breath evacuates my lungs in a *whoosh* when his hand delves between my thighs and thick fingers skim my pussy.

"Callan has asked that we have a family dinner tomorrow. His mother is in town." His tone doesn't match the message he's delivering. It's too gruff—thick sounding. Astor's voice like this is quickly becoming my favorite thing. It has a weird way of calming me but making me nervous at the same time. "You will be joining us."

It will be hard enough to look Callan in the eyes knowing I'm fucking his *father*, but now I'm supposed to sit across from him at a table and enjoy a meal...while his *mother* is there.

A *nightmare*...I've found myself in a complete and utter nightmare, and I only have myself to blame. I *chose* this.

The only thing stopping me from freaking the fuck out over these impromptu dinner plans are Astor's fingers. My hips roll, greedily begging for more as he massages my clit.

"Does that feel good?" he growls into my ear.

My head nods in jerky movements.

"Words, Indie." I suck in a deep breath as Astor pinches my clit between his fingers. A clear warning. "I want to hear your words."

"Yes, it feels good."

He rewards me by restarting the slow circles, this time increasing the pressure. As I proved to him, I can come by my own fingers, but I think I much prefer his.

"Do you want me to get you off like this? Right here on my deck where anyone on the lake could see us?" His words send shocks right to my core, making my pussy throb even more.

"Yes, please."

I'm not sure what I expect him to do, but to pull away completely, leaving me on the brink of an orgasm isn't it. My mewl of frustration and disappointment is involuntary and immediate.

"I want you to answer my fucking calls. Regardless of whatever predicament you've found yourself in. That was the vow you made to me when you agreed to be mine. You ignored my messages today and for that you're going to be punished." The sound of his zipper lowering has my head turning back toward him. "You think I'd forgotten how our day started?"

My mouth waters at the sight of his pants lowering and his thick cock being freed.

"Get on your knees for me, pretty girl," he commands sinisterly. "You're going to choke on my cock and fucking thank me when you're done."

TWELVE
INDIE

CALLAN WALKS out of Astor's office, a perplexed look on his face as he stalks toward me. My stomach drops and my heart rate rapidly picks up when his hand wraps around my arm. Without a word, he drags me away from the spot in the hallway I'd been loitering in while he talked with his dad.

When Callan showed up to the house twenty minutes ago and found me sitting at the kitchen island, drinking the iced green tea the chef had made for me. With one look at him, I knew Astor hadn't bothered to inform him of my new living situation yet. Why Astor would wait until *tonight* at this family dinner to inform him, I don't know. I want to call him out on it, but my jaw still hurts from the last punishment I received. I'm not complaining though, I found I enjoyed the way he commanded my head and ability to breathe last night on the deck. There was something absolutely exhilarating about it.

I didn't get a chance to so much as say hello to Callan before Astor appeared in the doorway as if out of thin air. I'm tempted to tie a bell on the man, I swear.

"My office. Now." Astor had commanded his son, disappearing down the hall again a second later. Callan stared at me for a moment as if he was trying to find the answers written across my forehead before following after his dad.

My plan wasn't to hide out in the hallway outside Astor's home office, but when I heard the staff greet Callan's mother, June, I darted out of the kitchen before I was forced to face her alone.

Callan's legs are much longer than mine and I struggle to keep up with his fast pace. He finally stops once we reach the sitting room at the front of the house. Everything in this room is white and pristine. A red wine lover's worst nightmare. I feel like I'm staining something just by standing in here.

"Why didn't you tell me about what your mother did?" Callan questions in a low whisper.

The scowl on his face reminds me so much of the expression his father constantly makes. They look similar with their lean muscles and tall frames, but I get the feeling Callan takes more after his mother. His eyes are deep blue where Astor's are gray, and Callan's brown hair is shades lighter than Astor's ever was. I'm quite fond of the silver strands starting to grow on Astor's temples now.

"You should have called me, Indie," he continues, not giving me a chance to speak. "I could have helped you pack. Dad says she only gave you an hour to collect as much as you could."

I was curious to know just how much Astor had told Callan, but the fact that Callan is only talking about my abrupt eviction, I think it's safe to assume that his dad didn't give him the full background of my shitshow life. And he *definitely* didn't inform him about our little arrangement.

With a yank, I free my arm from Callan's grip. "I did call you, Callan," I snap at him between clenched teeth. "But just like the rest of my recent messages to you lately, my call yesterday went unanswered."

I didn't know what to do after my mother showed up at my door yesterday. The panic and fear of what was going to happen next had me reaching out for something familiar. It's for the best Callan didn't answer. An hour after my missed call to him, I realized I didn't truly want him there. I just didn't want to be alone in that moment.

The frustration melts from Callan's face and guilt appears in its place. "I'm sorry." He steps back, awkwardly rubbing the back of his neck. "I was out of town for a couple of days, and I've been... busy."

"*Out of town?* Where did you—" I start to ask but decide halfway through that I don't actually care. What's going on in Callan's life no longer concerns me. Just like what's happening in mine doesn't concern him. "I get you've been busy, but I'm just making a point." I shift my weight to one foot and cross my arms in front of me. "I've been trying to call you for almost two weeks so we could talk."

He nods. "I know. It actually works out really well that you're here tonight because the same thing I need to talk to my parents about, I was going to tell you later." He squeezes my shoulder, and a soft smile lifts his lips. "But let's talk just the two of us after dinner."

"Okay," I agree, wanting to get this over with as soon as possible.

"Come on, I'll introduce you to my mother."

His mother and my lover's *ex-wife*.

Oh, *joy*.

Maybe I can get out of this dinner early by stabbing myself with one of the many salad forks I saw on the elaborately set table earlier.

YOU KNOW when you meet someone new and within two minutes of your introduction, you know that if they were ever on fire, instead of saving them, you'd roast a marshmallow in the flames?

That's how I feel about the ex-wife.

From the very start of our evening, she's looked at me as if I were the gum beneath her shoe. Her judgmental eyes raked over me, picking out all the things she didn't like. I could practically *hear* her thoughts as she created false little notions about me in her head. If it weren't for the excessive amount of Botox and filler in her face, I'm sure I would be able to see them written in her expressions too. The permanent scowl on her face is the only one I've received. Because of this, I don't know if Callan has her smile, but I was right in thinking he got his eye color from her.

"Tell me again what you're studying, Andie?" She squints at me from across the large table while dabbing the corners of her mouth with her cloth napkin.

"*Indie*," Astor corrects, not bothering to look at her as he does.

For the most part, Astor hasn't given her the time of day. While she seemed thrilled to see him, he barely acknowledged her. The few times his gaze has flicked in her direction, it's as if he's looking through her. Like he's blocking her very existence out. It's a skill I'm thinking took years of practice to master.

"Oh, my apologies, dear," the false sincerity all but drips off her over-filled lips. "Maybe if my son had bothered to discuss you and your relationship during our phone calls, I'd be better prepared and remember your name."

The fact that he'd never bothered to tell his own mother about me after all this time proves that we were never meant to be more than fleeting figures in each other's lives. If I ever really mattered to him, my name would have come up in conversation before tonight.

Sitting directly next to her, Callan sighs, head shaking. "Mom, come on, please. I asked for *one* dinner together. Just one where someone didn't act like an ass."

"Are you calling me an *ass*, Callan Banes?"

If it walks and bitches like a duck...

Callan rubs his temple like he's already getting a headache. Seems neither one of us won the mother lottery.

"No, that's not what I'm saying..." he trails off, giving up the fight.

Deciding to take pity on him, I clear my throat, regaining the woman's attention. "I want to be a nurse practitioner, so I'm working on my bachelors in nurse science. When I'm done with that, I'll need to get my masters."

Underneath the table, Astor's fingertips begin to trace circles on my bare thigh. I want to look at him but drawing attention to ourselves is the last thing we need to do at this already hostile table. Even when his movements start to travel upward, I force myself to remain still.

"That sounds like a lot of schooling," June comments, feigning interest.

My thighs involuntarily squeeze tighter when Astor's fingers attempt to pry them apart. The tightening of his grip on my skin is my silent warning. *Do not deprive me.*

"I'm only nineteen," I explain, my voice sounding surprisingly even despite my growing flustered state. Ever so slowly, I part my legs for Astor as I add, "I'm not too worried about it."

"Are you taking any summer classes like Callan? Those extra credits really helped expedite his time at university. Which I think is for the best, personally. It's time he joined the real world." June's hand rubs Callan's shoulder, a gesture neither one of them look entirely comfortable with.

From the corner of my eyes, I can see Astor's lips pull in the slightest smirk when he finds I'm not wearing underwear again. He told me to wear the same thing as yesterday for tonight's dinner. I just assumed he meant the *exact* same, so I forwent panties again.

Callan clears his throat and shifts in his seat. "That's actually what I wanted to talk to you guys about tonight."

Pulling on my leg again, I'm forced to subtly shift in my chair so I can widen to Astor's desired position. Nothing about Astor's tone or posture gives away what's taking place under the table. He's as cool and composed as always. Meanwhile, I think my pounding heart might break a rib.

"You wanted to have this dinner together so we could talk about your summer courses?" Astor questions.

"No," Callan corrects. "I actually wanted to let you all know that I've already completed all the credits I need to graduate. I've been busy working and talked to my advisors, and they all agree that I can graduate a semester early. I'll officially be done in December."

June's proud cheering and congratulatory words muffle out the sharp gasp that escapes my lips as Astor's fingers graze my exposed pussy. He's teasing—*no, preparing* me for what he has intended. The fact he requested I wear this damn dress shows that this is something he *planned* for. This isn't a spur of the moment kind of thing. Real thought went into this.

"That's excellent news, Callan," he praises his son with a nod of his head while languidly tracing up and down my seam. "I know this is a goal you've had since high school. I'm proud of you for accomplishing it."

"Thanks, Dad." Callan looks at me next and my distracted brain quickly remembers I need to say something.

"I'm really happy for you, Callan." I truly mean it when I say it. My romantic feelings for him may have diminished, but I still want nothing but happiness and success for him. "You're going to do amazing things…" My words trail off when Astor teases my opening. "I just know it," I add tightly.

There's no way for me to know if the smile I give him looks as forced as it feels.

Astor pushes a finger inside me, and my chin falls to my chest in an attempt to conceal the shocked parting of my lips.

This isn't happening. He's not actually doing this while his son and ex sit across the table. The logical side of my brain tries to reason, but the increasing rhythm of his finger sliding in and out of me proves otherwise.

With a deep breath, I try to settle myself before lifting my head again.

"What are your plans for after you graduate?" June asks over her glass of expensive red wine. She'd requested Callan fetch one of the bottles from Astor's cellar before we sat down at the table like she still had a right to Astor's belongings.

Callan looks at me like he's about to deliver life altering news. It's not his intense expression that has my heartrate picking up. It's his father's palm grinding against my sensitive clit.

"I've spent the better part of the past three months getting everything in order, but as soon as I graduate in December, I'll be moving to New York." Finally, after months of secrets and Callan's illusive behavior, the truth is finally out. "I flew out there this week and met with uncle Emeric. He's offered to let me work for him." He looks at his dad when he delivers the last part. There's a glimmer of fear in his eyes, like he's afraid his dad won't approve of this career choice.

I've never heard Callan speak of Emeric before, so I have no idea what this job could entail, but by the way June's concrete face falls, I don't think it's good.

"*Emeric* as in your *brother?*" She says his name quietly as if she could accidentally summon the man here if spoken too loudly. "That doesn't seem wise. Astor, you'd allow this?"

The heal of Astor's palm grinds harder against me and at the same time he opens his mouth to speak, he slips another finger inside of me. It takes everything I have in me to not jolt at the intrusion. "Who am I to tell him no? Callan is a grown man. He must set his own path and he must learn to stand by the decisions he makes."

Starting at the top of my head, sparks of pleasure begin to shoot through my body. My skin is too warm and the muscles in my core are starting to quiver. With shaky fingers, I lay my hand over Astor's, silently begging him to stop so I don't come right here at this table.

My plea goes unanswered and has the opposite effect I'd hoped for. His tempo and pressure increase, the only thing holding back my orgasm is my sheer will.

Fuck. Fuck. Fuck.

"I think this could be a really good opportunity for me and there's so much I can learn from Bran—"

Knotting my hands in the fabric of my dress, I fly up from the table and away from Astor's relentless hand. Completely flustered, I breathlessly apologize to Callan for so rudely cutting him off. "I'm sorry, I—I will just be a moment."

With the briefest glance at Astor's smug face, I scurry out of the room before anyone has a chance to say anything else.

THIRTEEN
ASTOR

"I'M GOING to go select another bottle of wine from the cellar," I explain, removing my napkin from my lap and pushing away from the table.

Indie, along with her greedy cunt, are hiding somewhere from me. I want to be angry at her for leaving before I could make her come, but the fact I get to now go hunt her down like she's my prey excites me.

June taps her nearly empty glass. "Be a gem and grab another bottle of cabernet while you're down there, Astor."

The only reason I still tolerate June's presence is for Callan. No matter how strong my ill will is toward her, she will always be Callan's mother. And because of that, she will forever be a permanent burden in my life. That was her grand plan twenty-three years ago when she fell pregnant with our son. It was the oldest play in the books, and I still somehow fell victim to it.

I will never regret my son's existence, but I will regret how it came about for the remainder of my days.

Though, my biggest regret will always be allowing my father to persuade me into marrying the conniving woman. The Banes have an image to uphold and a baby out of wedlock was not something he would stand for. It wasn't until he was forcibly removed from power and cold and dead, did I divorce June. Our marriage came to an end just after three years, and not once during those three years did my dislike for her wane. Over two decades later, I enjoy her company even less.

I could acknowledge the fact she'd spoken to me, but I find it much more satisfactory to just ignore her completely. The fact my disregard for her presence irks her to no end only makes it that much sweeter.

Indie was desperate to get away from me. The sanctuary of her new bedroom would have been too far for her frazzled brain to consider running to. She would be looking for a much closer and accessible hideaway.

The soles of my dress shoes click against the hardwood floors as I stalk through the grand entryway and down the hallway that my office resides in. While I highly doubt she would be foolish enough to enter my office without permission, I still peek through the open door to be sure. I'm fairly good at anticipating her moves, but she's had a few moments where she's surprised me. Like yesterday on the deck where she enthusiastically choked on my cock. My punishment ended up bringing her more pleasure than I had intended.

Walking past the closed door of one of the bathrooms, I come to a stop when I hear water running. My smirk is instant and anticipation shoots through me like a bullet.

Found you, pretty girl.

My knuckles rap against the door.

The faucet turns off and there's a short pause before the voice comes through the wood door. "Just a minute."

We don't have a minute. If Callan or June decided to leave the formal dining room, questions I don't feel like answering would be asked.

I don't say anything, instead I knock once more.

She sighs in frustration before her footsteps move across the room. The sound of the lock turning has my blood rushing to my dick. *Finally.* The door isn't open more than an inch before I'm shoving my way into the bathroom.

Indie's eyes widen and lips part, her shriek is just barely silenced in time when my hand clamps down across her mouth. I shut the door again and lock us inside.

"Nowhere to run this time, Indie," I growl close to her face as I push her until her back hits the marble vanity. "You're trapped in here with me and you're going to stay here until I've had my fucking fill."

She tries to speak behind my hand.

"Shh," I coo, brushing the strands of her hair off her face. "We don't want anyone overhearing us, now do we? You cleverly chose to not wear panties, so I don't have anything to gag you with this time. If you're too loud, I'm going to be very disappointed in you."

Her breath comes faster, her breasts heaving out the top of her white sundress. She's nervous about being locked in here with me, but her dilating pupils and the way she arches into me gives away her readiness.

My free hand dips between her thighs. "I'm going to finish what I started," I tell her. "But this time, you're going to come on my cock."

Indie's eyes close involuntarily when I slip a finger back into her slick heat. She's wetter than she was when she left the table. My cock presses against the zipper of my slacks, eager to sink into her warmth.

"My pretty girl is ready for me, isn't she?"

She whimpers against my hand and her hips roll, grinding against my palm. Her movements are frantic—desperate even. My teasing from earlier has her eager for me.

Pulling my soaked finger from her core causes disappointment to flash across her face. It disperses when I use both hands to lift her onto the bathroom countertop.

Standing between her spread thighs, I order her, "Take my cock out."

Pushing my black cashmere sweater up, Indie's deft fingers tackle the button and zipper of my charcoal slacks. The entire time, I watch how she bites her bottom lip. I've never been fond of the act of kissing. Somehow the act felt more intimate than fucking, but there's a pull in my chest urging me to kiss Indie now. My teeth grind and I suppress the unwanted desire.

She shoves my pants down on my hips, allowing my cock to spring free. Her lips twitch as she looks up at me. "Seems I'm not the only one going commando tonight, Mr. Banes."

"I told you I like easy access." I smirk. "Spit on me. Get my cock ready for your pussy."

Her thin fingers wrap around my thick shaft, and I watch, completely enthralled, as the saliva drips from her lips onto the tip of my dick. My hips jerk forward at her first languid stroke. Tip to base, she spreads the wetness over me.

I drop my forehead against hers. This close, it's like we're sharing oxygen. My other hand wraps around her wrist, halting her movements. "Wrap your legs around my waist."

Pulling her ass to the very edge of the counter, she does what I ask. The heels of her feet dig into my lower back, and she pulls me in closer to her center. Her head falls back against the mirror behind her as I glide my dick through her soaked lips. The head grazes over her sensitive clit, making her whole body jolt.

Her eyes plead with me when I position myself at her entrance.

"*Please.*" It's just barely an audible whisper, but still hearing that singular word come from her lips is one of my favorite sounds.

I'm just about to grant her wish when the knock comes at the door. "Indie?"

At the sound of Callan's voice, Indie flies forward and tries to jump from the vanity. My hands lock around her thighs in a punishing grasp, forcing her to stay in place. Pure fear shines in her amber orbs.

My only answer is a slow shake of my head, a devious grin growing on my lips. I couldn't have planned this better if I tried. Dropping my head close to hers, I speak lowly into her ear. "Answer him, Indie."

Body still rigid, I push her back until she rests against the mirror once more. Her eyes flick between where my cock slides through her pussy again and the door her boyfriend stands behind.

When she doesn't answer, my fingers flex on her skin in warning.

Finally, she finds her words. "I—I'm here." Her response comes out cracked, as if her throat is clogged with emotion.

I know the truth, but Callan doesn't. "Are you okay? You sound upset," he asks, sounding worried. It's a little too late for him to be concerning himself with Indie's emotions.

Indie looks at me for help and I simply mouth a single word.

Lie.

"Yes, I'm okay." Her breath shudders when I position myself at her opening again. The subtle shake of her head is her silent plea, and a wicked smile is my reply. "I just needed a minute to —" She loses the ability to breathe and speak as the head of my cock pushes into her. "—to collect myself," she manages to finish.

Her back arches as I push inch by inch into her and her fingernails dig into the top of my hands that still hold her thighs open.

"Are you sure?" Callan presses.

Again, I whisper in her ear, but this time I slice all the way into her as I speak. "*Lie better.*"

She licks her bottom lip before responding. "There's just so many things going on right now, Callan. Between my mom and you, I just need a second to process."

I'm proud of her ability to keep her voice even. There's only the slightest quiver in her speech, but I think it's only noticeable to me because I'm causing it. My thrusts are slow and measured to keep the sound at a minimum, but they're deep, brushing against her womb.

The open mouth kisses I trail across her jaw are her reward for her job well done, but Callan is relentless. "I'm sorry I told you tonight instead of earlier. I wanted to make sure everything was set in stone before I told you. Open the door and we can talk about this."

"No!" Indie instantly snaps, head whipping in the direction of the locked door. "I mean…I'll be out soon. Please just give me a minute and I'll find you so we can finally talk about things."

There's a long pause before Callan answers, "Okay. I'll be on the deck waiting for you."

Indie doesn't fully relax until there's the audible sound of footfalls leaving. Once they become distant, her body sags in relief. "Holy fuck," she breathes.

"Such a good girl," I growl in approval, my hips driving into her faster. The restraint I've been relying on all night vanishing each time her core muscles clench around me. "*My* good girl."

"Yes," she agrees with a long moan. "*Yours.*"

Indie can deny that she didn't enjoy our secret games tonight, but the way her body has been responding to me would give away her falsehoods. She likes the threat of being caught, it exhilarates her and turns her on just as it does me. The blood in my veins is basically made of fire at his point.

Indie's breath begins to come in short pants. I would have normally told her to keep her hands on the marble counter, but I find I'm enjoying how they restlessly travel over my arms and chest. When I press my thumb to her clit, her nails prick the back of my neck, making a low groan form in my throat.

Tingles begin to form at the base of my spine and my balls

tighten. My teeth sink in my lip and my rhythm becomes erratic as I chase my release.

It's Indie that comes apart first. My hand slaps across her mouth, muffling her cries of ecstasy just before white-hot pleasure blazes through me like fireworks going off.

Thrusting deep, I spill inside of her with a harsh curse.

I stay buried in her as we both fight to regain our breaths. My head drops to Indie's shoulder and her skin feels sticky against mine.

I get lost in the soft circles she trails through the cropped strands on my scalp. Prickles dance across my skin. It's a soothing gesture that feels borderline too intimate for our kind of relationship. I allow it for a minute before standing straight.

The flush across Indie's cheeks is a stunning red and the sheen of sweat across her forehead was well earned. Her lips part in a silent gasp as my still semi-hard dick slips out of her sensitive center.

My eyes fixate on the way my cum trickles out of her, finding pleasure that I've found another way to mark her as mine.

Indie's eyes widen as my thumb collects what's fallen out and pushes it back inside of her.

"What are you doing?"

"While you break up with my son, I want my cum dripping out of you."

FOURTEEN
INDIE

THE CHILLY NIGHT air does little to cool my heated skin as I step out onto the deck. Just like he said he would, Callan is leaning against the railing waiting for me. He doesn't immediately turn to me when the door closes behind me. His eyes are scanning the dark lake below us, but I know he hears me approach by the way he stands up straighter.

The anxious feeling building in my chest feels like a band that is slowly constricting my lungs. I know I need to say something to him, but I'm afraid of what might come out of my mouth. My mind is still frazzled from my encounter with Astor and I'm not thinking clearly. The fact that Astor was right, and I can, indeed, feel him seeping out of me isn't helping matters either.

What's funny though, is that I'm not dreading having this conversation with Callan. It's one that's been months in the making and it's long past due that we had it. What scares me is that with one look at my flushed cheeks, Callan will know my secret. I don't know if or when Callan will learn what is happening here, but I don't think telling him tonight is a good idea. Especially not when his *mother* is still here, filling the house up with judgmental stares and her too-strong floral perfume.

No, all we need to do tonight is call time of death on our nonexistent relationship so we can both freely move on.

"Are you going to miss it?" I ask once I find my ability to string words together. "You've lived in Washington your whole life. It can't be easy to walk away."

There's a brief pause followed by a sigh before Callan turns to me. "It's something I should have done a long time ago, but I put it on the backburner and tried to continue with my life here. I know now going to New York is the right thing for me. Everything I want is there and I've just been avoiding it."

I can't help but think there's more meaning behind his words than he's letting on. What else is in New York other than his uncle and this new job?

Stepping next to him, I mirror his posture and lean against the railing. "I just want you to be happy, Callan. Whether that's here or in New York." My hand rests over his. "And I know for a fact I'm not the person that makes you happy."

His lips part like he's going to argue with me, but I'm quick to cut him off.

"No, it's okay," I promise. "It's okay because the roles we were meant to play in each other's lives, we've played them to their fullest extent. This is where we end. There's nothing else for us to do and there's nothing left for us to give. If we had more to give, we wouldn't be having this conversation. The one thing you will *always* have, whether you're here or across the country, is my friendship. *That* will never change or waver."

He stares at me, head softly shaking. "I haven't been fair to you, Indie. I entered this relationship knowing that I'd never be able to give you more, that this wasn't for the long haul. It wasn't fair to let you think even for a minute that we'd be more than we were."

It's weird. This admission should hurt, right? My heart

should break at least a little knowing he never wanted more, but it doesn't. I think it's because, deep down, I always knew that we were never more than brief shiny sparks in each other's lives. Our light dimmed fast, but that's how it was fated to be.

"We both knew it wasn't going to work. There was always an expiration date on this." I was blinded by the thrill of him at first and didn't want to see what was inevitably lying in front of us. But it became painfully obvious to me this summer when we drifted apart and neither one of us seemed to care. We've been living our own separate lives for months.

"The truth is, I wanted this to work," he admits, shocking me. "I realize now that my reasons were purely selfish. Which is again why I was never fair to you, and I'm genuinely so sorry."

There's not a hint of a lie when I say, "I believe you, and please don't apologize to me. It's truly not needed." *I'm* the one massively in the wrong here. I mean, for fuck's sake, his *father's* cum is running down my inner thigh as we're having this nice little heart to heart.

Like he's suddenly nervous, he pulls his hand out from under mine so he can use it to anxiously rub the back of his neck. "I feel like …" he trails off, still unsure of himself. "I feel like I owe you more, I don't know, *honesty*. There's more that I need to tell you."

My head shakes at this and my own guilt creeps up my throat. "You really don't owe me anything, Callan. We're good." *Please don't tell me more because then I'm going to feel like I need to do the same.*

"No, I need to tell you. I promised her I would."

"*Her?*"

His handsome face pinches. "Yeah. Her."

Just like that, it makes sense. All the unspoken words from tonight appear and fall into place. The missing pieces for his need to be in New York fill in all the blanks and I suddenly feel like I'm seeing the full picture. And I finally feel like I'm seeing and understanding Callan Banes.

"What's her name?" My smile is genuine when I ask. I want to know about the girl that has such a strong hold on his heart that he's picking up everything and moving across the country.

He's thrown for a second by my lack of anger; I can tell by the way a vast array of emotions reflect in his eyes in a short time frame. Callan hesitates like he's worried my curiosity is masking an ulterior motive. It's like he thinks I'm playing it cool to only go off on him once I have all the information.

"I meant what I said, Callan. I want you to be happy and if she's the one who makes you happy, how can I be angry at you for that?" I try to assure him.

He exhales a long breath. "I couldn't love you the way you deserved to be loved because I've been in love with Ophelia since I was fifteen years old. There's a lot of history between us and a lot of mistakes were made on my part, but I won't get into that now. It just comes down to this; I tried to move on and for a split second I let myself believe I could do that with you. No matter how hard I tried, I couldn't and again, I'm sorry for that."

"Stop apologizing to me." It's not a request, it's a demand. How can I accept an apology from him when I can't tell him the truth about my own wrongdoings? "Did you know that she was in New York when you decided to work with your uncle?"

"I knew she was attending NYU, but I hadn't planned to seek her out yet, but then she was just *there*. I was out to dinner with Emeric and a colleague, and she just appeared. Ophelia was as shocked as I was. Like I said, there's a lot of history there, but we've spent some time together during my visits out there." His blue eyes flick to mine. "I slept with her, Indie."

"I figured you had." I offer him a soft smile with a shrug. "This whole thing sounds like fate to me. I don't know why we'd even try to fight against that. Watching my dad die when he hadn't even lived half a life put things into perspective for me.

Fight for the things you want and let go of the things that are no longer serving you." I reach out and grip his forearm. "You can let go, Callan, knowing there isn't any animosity between us, and I'll do the same."

He still looks unsure. "*Really*? You're not mad at me for cheating?"

I can't help but laugh at this. "No, I'm not mad at you. Is it really considered cheating when we haven't touched each other in months, and we don't talk anymore? We parted ways long ago, we just haven't verbally acknowledged it."

"I guess that's true." There's a long pause before he asks a question that makes my heart lurch in my throat. "Have you slept with anyone else?"

My first instinct is to lie, but instead I ask, "Would you be mad if I had?"

His response is immediate. "Not even a little bit. I want the same for you, Indie. I want you to move on and be happy."

My guilt lessens but doesn't completely fade. No, that won't go anywhere until the full truth is on the table. "Are you, Callan? Are you happy?"

A look crosses his face that I can't quite decipher. I think it might be doubt. I don't think I've ever seen him wear such an emotion. He's always seemed so sure of himself. For some reason, the fact that Ophelia can make him feel unsteady makes me happy. Callan needs someone like that—someone who will keep him on his toes and challenge him.

"There's still a lot that I need to fix between us, and I have a feeling it'll be an uphill battle for me, but I also know that it'll all be worth it if it works out."

Stepping forward, I wrap my arm around his middle in a light hug. "Go to New York and fight for your happiness. I'll be here cheering you on the whole time."

Callan hugs me back. "I didn't deserve you, but you're going to find someone who does, and they'll see just how amazing you are. You truly are one of a kind, Indie, and I'm thankful for the time we had."

I don't know what it says about me—and my money's on *not good things*—but I find myself silently thanking him for putting Astor in my life. Without Callan, I would have no idea what it's like to have Astor ignite pieces of me I didn't know existed and then have him put out the flames with his tongue.

FIFTEEN
ASTOR

THERE'S AN ODD, almost primitive, feeling growing in my chest knowing the strings that tethered her to another man are currently being severed. After tonight, she truly will be completely and solely *mine*. No one but me will have a claim to her. It makes the selfish and possessive side of me purr with satisfaction.

I've shared women in the past, but not Indie. Never Indie.

She's all mine.

Footsteps moving toward the den have my eyes lifting from the amber liquid in my glass. Callan leans against the doorframe, legs crossed casually at his ankles. He looks at me like he's not sure what he wants to say, so I speak first.

"It's always been her, hasn't it?" I take a drink of the scotch and savor the burn.

He has to know that I've kept tabs on Ophelia's whereabouts through the years. At his first mention of New York tonight, I knew she was his real motive for moving there.

His head nods without hesitation. "Yes."

There're very few people that know the history between Callan and the young girl that used to live next door, but I know all the details. I'm the one who had to pay off the judge and police department when things went south for them. The best thing that ever happened was when Ophelia's family moved away. And yet, after all these years, my son's affection for her never wavered.

"I suppose I should be commending you for your steadfast dedication to her. I can't help but be concerned though." My eyes narrow with a pointed stare. "Think carefully about your next steps, Callan. Like I told your mother, you are a man now and can make your own decisions. That also means that you need to be capable of cleaning up your own messes. I won't do it again. That goes for your doings with Ophelia *and* Emeric."

There's a sense of pride in my chest when he stands up taller and his face hardens. The determination and confidence he's showing is something he'll need if he's going to work for my brother—for the family business.

"I know what I'm doing and I'm ready."

"You say that now, but you truly have no idea what you're getting into. I've shielded you and kept you in the dark on a lot of the various *operations* that my family is involved in. Emeric won't shield you. He will throw you into the deep end with nothing more than a rusty pocketknife, and he'll laugh while he does it."

People like to say that my youngest brother and I couldn't be more different. What they don't know is that in our souls, we're very much the same. The horrible things that he's capable of doing? I'm the one who taught him how to execute them. There just came a point in my life that I didn't like the man I was becoming. I backed away from that world and became a scholar while Emeric embraced the darkness like an old lover.

My father is probably rolling in his grave knowing that I stepped away from the business to pursue a career in academics and left the empire in Emeric's hands. He is, after all, the better and *only* choice since my other brother joined the Navy and never looked back. I'm not even sure he's alive, if I'm being honest. I haven't seen him since he enlisted at the age of eighteen.

Callan doesn't back down. "I said I was ready. This is what I want to do, and I'm thankful I get to learn from Emeric."

I lift my glass in a salute-like fashion. "Then I wish you nothing but luck, kid."

"Thanks, but I really don't think I'll need it." And just like that, the cocky college boy I know so well returns. If he pulls this smug look with my brother, Emeric will beat it out of him.

My son is in for a rude awakening.

"I think you will. Especially if you're planning on reconnecting with Ophelia."

His lips pull, somehow making him appear more arrogant. "I don't think I'm the one who needs luck right now, Dad."

My head cocks ever so slightly. "What does *that* mean exactly?"

"It means you don't give me enough credit."

"I'm still not following you."

"One day soon, you will." His shoulder shrugs, and he moves away from the doorframe. "I need to go find Mom so I can get her out of here before she stirs up too much trouble. I think two hours once a year is enough family time, don't you?"

"I wouldn't mind if the next time we all got together was at a funeral. Hers or mine, I don't care. I'm not overly particular at this point."

Believing I'm joking, Callan's laugh follows him as he walks down the hallway.

SHE'S JUST STEPPING out of the shower and wrapping the white towel around herself when I find her. Freezing briefly in place like she's not sure about either of our next moves, she looks at me expectantly, like I somehow need to explain my presence in her room. I will do no such thing. This is my house and I'll go where I want, when I want.

Tucking the towel tighter, Indie closes the glass shower doors behind her and moves to the marble vanity. "Did Callan leave?" she asks, looking at me through the reflection in the mirror.

"He did." I step up behind her and skim my hands across her narrow shoulders and down her arms. My fingertips trail through the water droplets still covering her soft skin.

"We talked, ended things." She pauses, shaking her head with a soft chuckle. "It seems ridiculous to say that. We were already over. Our conversation—while I'm glad we had it—was just a formality."

"A needed formality." I didn't realize how much I craved her detaching herself from another man—even if that man is my son —until I knew she was completely free to be called mine.

Her head nods in agreement. "Did you know about his plans to move to New York before tonight?"

For a split second, my untamed jealousy shoots to the surface, thinking she's only asking because she still wants to be with him, but then she continues on, soothing the unwanted emotion.

"Sounds like it'll be good for him. I hope he can work things out with Ophelia. I'm a sucker for second chances and I hope they get theirs."

"I had my suspicions this was his plan. He's always been very inquisitive about the Bane family business and history, and he's always been fond of Emeric." Their connection started when Callan was only a toddler, and even when I moved us here to Seattle, Emeric kept in touch with my son.

Indie reaches for a bottle of moisturizer and dots the product across her face before massaging it into her blemish-free skin. "What exactly does your family do?"

"Aren't you an inquisitive one tonight?" My tone is sharper than I intend, and it has her eyes turning downcast.

"I'm sorry. You don't have to answer. I was just curious."

For a reason I can't seem to put my finger on, I find myself sighing and answering her question. Perhaps it's to wash away the look of remorse on her pretty face. "The Banes have had their hands in numerous pots for many decades. Some of us work in importing and exporting, and others get jobs in politics. We like to equally distribute our presence across many different fields. That way we retain some semblance of control in multiple industries. Keeps us informed and ahead of our competitors."

Her brows furrow. "That sounds ... intense. What will Callan be doing?"

"I think Emeric will have him putting his forensic accounting degree to use and dealing with the money. He'll probably start Callan off with the various nightclubs' finances and then move him up the chain from there." My hands continue to trace lines across her bare skin. I like the way goosebumps form in my wake.

"Your brother is going to have Callan looking for fraud and money laundering in his *own* businesses?"

I can't help but laugh at this. She's so innocent at times. Other times—times when I'm between her spread thighs and my cock is buried in her—she's delectably sinful.

"No, pretty girl, he'll be looking for ways to get away with fraud and laundering."

And just like that, it all clicks. Her pink lips form a silent 'oh' and her head nods in understanding. "*Gotcha.*" I expect her to say more, but instead, she shocks me when her amber eyes flick to mine with a smirk. "Now I know why you're the way you are. You could never just be a *scholar*. Your devious ways were weaved into your very DNA."

"I may have chosen a different career path than the rest of my family, but that doesn't change who I am."

Mischief shining in her eyes, she bites her bottom lip. "Good."

She continues to surprise me. Keeping my eyes locked with hers in the mirror, I press my lips to her shoulder. She smells good. Whatever shampoo or body soap she uses is sweet, reminding me of honey. My nose runs along her neck, and I breathe it in. "Did you wash away all the evidence of what I did to your body earlier?"

By the way her cheeks flush, Indie knows exactly what I'm talking about. "We haven't talked about it, but I'm on birth control. Just in case you were worried about ... you know ... knocking me up."

My fingers wrap around the wet strands of her hair, and I pull her head back, exposing her neck to me. "I know," I admit against her soft skin. "I saw the pill packet in your purse this summer."

"You went through my purse?" She sounds more amused than mad.

"I needed to know all I could about you so I would be ready for when I could finally call you mine."

SIXTEEN
INDIE

IT WAS scary being called into the principal's office in grade school and high school, but it's equal parts balls-out terrifying and exhilarating being called into the university president's office.

I awoke with a one sentence text on my phone. *Come to my office thirty minutes before your first class.* With all text messages, you must infer tone, but with his, I don't have to guess.

It's a direct—non-negotiable—*order*. One I can't refuse, even if I wanted to, and despite the fear, I don't want to. I want to see what he has planned for me. I want to know what new heights he plans on taking my body. I've been at his house for seven days now, and with each passing day I've already experienced so much with him.

Just like the last time I visited this office, I keep my head down and take the elevator up to the top floor, but unlike last time, the floor isn't still or quiet. There's a constant low hum of business taking place. Phones are ringing and people are going on with their workday. I always knew I didn't want to be locked up in an office space like this or in a cubicle, working a nine to five. The very idea of it sounded *miserable*. I enjoy teaching the young kids lessons at the barn, but I know I don't want to make a full-time career out of it. It needs to continue to be a passion, not a chore. I figured out I wanted to work at a hospital after my dad got sick. The nurse practitioner that was on my dad's team was the one who brought him the most joy and comfort. I wanted to be like her—I *do* want to be like her. And because of Astor, I still have a chance.

The redhead, Cheska, stands from her desk when she sees me approach. Her eyes dart around like she's looking for a plausible reason I'd be back here. "You're not on his schedule."

I shrug my shoulders apathetically. "He told me to come." And I *always* come when he demands it of me—in *and* out of bed.

Like a good guard dog, she's not about to back down. "He's currently on a call. I'll let him finish it up and then alert him that you are here."

"How much longer is the call?" I have to be in class in just over thirty minutes. While I don't want to ignore his order to be here, I also can't afford to miss this class. It's preparing us for a big test next week, and now that I have a second chance to get my degree, I'm not about to let my grades slip because Astor Banes is distracting me.

Cheska glances at the tablet in her hand. "It says he'll be done around noon."

"That's over an hour from now."

It's her turn for her shoulders to lift. "Sorry. I'm not sure there's anything else I can do for you. I suppose you can leave him a note and I can pass it along when he's finished."

My phone is already in my hand, and I turn my attention to it while I respond to her, "I actually don't need you to do anything for me."

Indie: I'm here.

It takes less than ten seconds for his response to appear on my screen.

Astor: I'll come retrieve you.

Cheska's lips part in shock when Astor appears in the small reception area a moment later. "Mr. Banes, I thought you were on a call. I would have brought her to you had I known otherwise."

His gray eyes flick to her briefly. "Next time she's here, deliver her promptly to my office regardless of what my schedule says."

Looking and sounding confused, she stammers a quick, "Yes, sir."

Astor holds his arm out, silently gesturing for me to walk ahead of him to his large office. Remembering the way, I lead us, and while I do, I can feel my skin growing warm as his intense gaze rakes me from behind.

Once inside and with the doors closed behind us, I shuffle nervously to the leather chair I sat in last time. I'm about to sit down when his sharp command stops me in my tracks.

"No." Astor moves to his side of the desk and takes a seat in the leather desk chair. "You won't be sitting this time."

My hands flex around the strap of my shoulder bag while my core muscles instinctually clench.

"*Oh?*" I question, placing my bag and oversized plaid blazer on the chair in front of me. "And what will I be doing?"

The devious shine in his eyes is enough to make my knees weak. "You'll be getting your virgin ass ready to take my fat cock."

The mixture of fear and excitement that has been lingering in my veins amplifies tenfold. Before now, I've never had strong feelings one way or another regarding anal. I've never been opposed to it, but I definitely didn't seek it out. I assumed I'd figure out my feelings toward it when the moment happened.

And now that the moment is here, I can't help but be terrified of the unknown.

At my silent, taken aback expression, Astor continues to seal my fate. "I told you the last time you were in this office that I was going to be the first to claim you there. Did you think I was lying?"

"No," I choke out. "I'm just ..."

His head cocks. "Just *what*, Indie?"

My teeth dig painfully into my bottom lip as the blood rushes to my face and an embarrassed blush blooms. "I'm just scared it's going to hurt."

The intensity in his gaze dims a notch, and an almost, I don't know, *reassuring* look appears. "While I have every intention of fucking your ass, I also intend on making you enjoy it as much as I do." He pulls a drawer open on his desk and retrieves a black box. Wordlessly, he pushes it toward me and nods his head at it, signaling for me to open it.

With slightly shaky fingers, I lift the lid and examine the contents.

Looking up from the silver butt plug and bottle of lube, I ask, "You're going to put this inside me?"

He nods his head once. "Yes, and next week we're going to use a larger one. We're going to stretch your tight ass until you can take my cock comfortably." He pushes back in his chair, creating space between him and his desk. "Now, get over here so we can begin. We don't want you being late for class now, do we?"

On my next inhale, I hold it, and as I exhale it slowly through parted lips, I gather up all the courage I can. Everything else he's done to my body, I've thoroughly enjoyed. This should be no different, right? Before I can chicken out, I walk to Astor. Not knowing where he wants me exactly, I stand awkwardly in front of him.

"Other way." His large hands grip my hips and turn me to

face his desk. "Just like that first night I fucked you, I want you bent over in front of me."

Leaning forward, I rest my elbows and forearms on the desk. This position causes my short black pleated skirt to rise up, which I suspect was his intended goal.

Unable to stop it, I jolt when his fingers skim across my thighs as he pushes the fabric further up so he can see all of me. My thin black thong is doing little to conceal anything at this point.

"I really do appreciate your preference for skirts and dresses."

"Well, I do aim to please, Mr. Banes." My sarcastic retort is brought on by nerves, but the sharp slap across my right ass cheek is quick to thwart any further remarks.

"Oh, and how you please me so." I can't see him but by the way I can feel his breath across my skin, I suspect he's close. My theory is proven correct as his teeth scrape across my skin. It's not hard enough to leave a mark.

My heart speeds up when his fingers hook around the thin fabric of my thong, and he drags it down my legs. Instead of removing them completely, he allows them to remain around my ankles. Astor's hand slips between my thighs, forcing me to widen my stance another inch or so.

At the first brush of his finger across my clit, my whole body jolts and my hands tighten into fists. Astor's touch has a way of making me go from zero to painfully horny in a matter of seconds. With one look or one darkly spoken word, he has me aching for him.

Now is no different.

He takes his time creating slow, methodical circles with his finger and when my body has responded enough to his liking, his finger pushes inside my slick heat with ease. He works it in and out, thoroughly coating himself in my wetness before his finger travels upward to my virgin hole. Astor's fingertip traces over it and at the first hint of him applying light pressure, I find every one of my muscles tightening up.

Astor makes a chastising *tsking* noise. "That won't do now, will it? You're going to let me in, and I don't care how long it takes. You have to relax for me."

Easier said than done, right?

On a long exhale, I try to force my muscles to give up the fight, but it's not happening as effectively as I'd like. My body still feels tense—on edge—about what's to come.

"Let me help you."

His other hand that had been resting on my hip wraps around and picks up where his other left off. The second his fingers begin to strum against my clit, it's like a switch being flipped. My muscles melt into the desk and into him. His pace is steady and unrelenting—a clear mission in mind. Within a minute, I can feel the electric buzz forming under my skin as my orgasm builds.

While I focus on the building sensation, Astor uses this opportunity to push his fingertip into my ass. The small intrusion is foreign and feels like it's borderline too much for me to handle. I can't imagine what it'll feel like to have his whole cock inside me. How could he possibly fit there when his finger feels like it barely does?

"Oh god," I groan as he pumps the digit in and out ever so slightly.

His movements are small, but everything feels amplified there. Nerve endings that have never been ignited are awakened. Surprisingly, as my body adjusts to the new sensation, I find I don't hate it. No, quite the opposite.

I *like* it.

"Does this feel good?" I swear, Astor Bane's gruff voice is my own aphrodisiac. It heightens the euphoric bliss his hands and body create. "You're doing so good, pretty girl."

The rush of pleasure that I've barely been holding at bay

crashes into me. In order to stop myself from yelling out and alerting everyone to what we're doing in here, my teeth bite down into my bare forearm. I'm blind to whatever pain I might be causing as I ride the tidal wave of my orgasm. Neither one of Astor's hands let up as I do, but when I come back down a moment later, his hands are gone.

Panting heavily, I remove my teeth from my arm and rest my forehead against the cool surface of his desk. My relaxed state is interrupted when something cool dribbles down the crack of my ass.

At my startled jump, Astor runs a hand down my back. "It's just some lube. You're doing so well already, but this will make it easier for you to accept the plug." His reassuring words are accompanied by his finger once more pushing into me, methodically coating the virgin hole with lubricant. "My good girl can take anything I give her. Soon you're going to take my cock here and you're going to wonder why you were ever afraid."

I hear him reach into the same box he'd retrieved the lube from, and seconds later, cool metal slips through my pussy lips. He covers it in my wetness before bringing it upward. My heart is pounding in my chest, making the blood hum in my ears as my nerves return with new force.

Astor presses the plug against my asshole, and when he's met with resistance, he takes me by utter surprise when I feel him press hot kisses to the apex of each of my ass cheeks. "You can take it, Indie."

With his encouragement, my body relaxes once more. His single finger felt large, but the plug feels gigantic. The tight muscle fights the intrusion for only a second before it slips fully inside.

"Oh fuck," I moan against the arm that now bears bite marks. "So full."

"You think you're full now? Just wait till my cock is buried in you." Astor presses against the base of the plug, making me squirm. "Hell, I might fuck your pussy with that pink vibrator of yours just so you can fully understand the meaning of being *full*."

I'm about to ask him how he knows what color my vibrator is and if he'd gone through my things at the house when he pulls my thong back up into place and returns my skirt to its proper placement.

Utterly confused as to what is happening, I turn around with wide eyes and shaky muscles to face him. With each movement, I can feel the foreign object inside of me.

"What are you doing?" I question, falling over my words only a little bit.

Astor looks at his silver Rolex and then back at me. "I have a meeting in ten minutes, and you need to be on your way so you don't miss your class."

My eyes widen. "You mean … you're not taking it out?"

He sits back in his rolling chair, arms relaxed casually over the armrests. "No, and neither will you. You're going to go to your classes and go about your day as normal, and I will remove it myself later tonight." His grey, storm-like eyes clash into mine. "Every time you sit down or fucking move today, I want you to be reminded that not only do I own your cunt but I also own your ass."

SEVENTEEN
INDIE

"ONE OF MY connections checked out the lot of horses being sent into Canada. She saw a black thoroughbred there, but she can't be sure if it was Jupiter. The man running the lot wasn't interested in letting her get close to the animal, let alone rescue it. Or any of the other horses there, for that matter. He's holding out, seeing if we can put together more money to free them."

There are very few legitimate establishments in the states that sell and ship horses across the borders to be slaughtered, but each one of them is run by the scum of the earth. They see dollar signs, not living, breathing animals. So, of course, he's running a hard bargain.

I've been trying to keep my hopes low, but Tessa's update right now has all but made my hope go out the window. It's already been so long since anyone has laid eyes on my precious stallion. At this point, we're grasping at straws and clinging to the remnants of our silent wishes that he's still alive.

"In two weeks, we are headed there ourselves and I'll look for him with my own eyes, Indie. If Jupiter is there, I will bring him home to you. That's a promise I can keep. For you and your father." Tessa is trying to keep my spirits high but I'm feeling completely defeated.

"Thank you, Tess." I fight the burn forming in my throat as tears threaten to fall. "Talk to you soon."

Tessa says her goodbyes and the call disconnects.

I have multiple assignments due this week and I'd planned on working on them tonight, but after that phone call, all I want to do is crawl into bed for the night. Astor said this morning before he left my room after our morning sex fest that he had a dinner meeting and he'd be home late. While he's out, I suppose I can watch mindless TV and try to forget about Jupiter. A couple hour reprieve would be nice.

I'd stay out here on his back deck but the weather is starting to change and it's a little bit too chilly for that. I'm about to stand up from the wooden patio chair when my phone buzzes in my lap. Thinking it'll be Tessa again, I anxiously answer the phone, not bothering to look at the caller ID, but the voice on the other side takes me by surprise.

"Hello?"

"Hey, Indie."

I sit up straighter in my chair. "*Callan*? You're *calling* me? You never called me when we *were* dating, but *now* you are?"

"I know, the irony isn't lost on me either, but I actually need to ask you a favor. Will you be at the house tomorrow? The present I got my dad should be delivered then and someone needs to sign for it." His voice is slightly muffled by the sound of loud street noises, like he's in a city standing on a sidewalk or something. He's probably back in New York.

"Umm …" I think about my schedule tomorrow. "I don't have classes tomorrow, but I do have to be at the barn for a couple lessons around four."

"Perfect, the confirmation said it should be delivered before then. Thanks, Indie."

I stand up from the chair and head through the glass doors.

"Is his birthday tomorrow?" Astor has access to my school files and all kinds of other information. Meanwhile, I'm in the dark for the most part when it comes to him.

"No, it's Friday." I hear him mumble something to someone else, but I can't make out what he says.

"Will you be here for it?" If they're going to be here celebrating Astor's birthday, I don't think I need to be here. Maybe I can call Lark and go do something with her so I don't intrude on their day. It might be weird for me to be there. I'm not family, and I wouldn't really consider myself a friend either.

"What? No. We've never really celebrated his birthday together. We just exchange gifts and call it a day."

My heart sinks hearing this. Birthdays were always a big deal at my house—or they were when my dad was alive. He always went above and beyond for me on that day, and it makes me sad that no one does the same for Astor.

"Oh ... okay," I mutter, a plan already formulating in my head. Whether it's a good one is yet to be known. "Don't worry about your gift, I'll take care of it."

"Thank you, Indie."

I stare at the dark screen after I hang up and think about my next moves. My assignments are long forgotten and my sorrow for Jupiter is momentarily lessened now that I have a real task in front of me.

Everyone should have their birthday celebrated, and Astor Banes is no different. What's funny is I want to do this. I want to celebrate the man who swept me up in this turbulent and uncontrollable storm.

EIGHTEEN
ASTOR

ALL I WANT to do as I walk through the doors of my house is take a shower and find my girl and fuck her until we both fall asleep.

My day started with an early meeting and ending with a dinner meeting that ran an extra hour because some people just don't know when to stop talking. When the business portion of a meeting is done, I'm ready to leave. I don't find it necessary to stay and chat about things like their daughter's dance recital or how their ailing relative is doing. Those things don't concern me, nor do they *interest* me, but alas, sometimes we just have to play the part to maintain business relationships. No matter how tedious the task.

Removing my sports coat—still damp from the rain outside—I begin to ascend the grand staircase to go in search of Indie, but sounds coming from the kitchen have me pausing and changing course. The housekeeper is long gone for the day and the chef I have on hand didn't work today as I ate all my meals out. Meaning the object of my obsession isn't waiting in her room for me like she usually is.

Stalking further into the house, my blood all but hums at the anticipation of touching her. I hear Indie before I see her, and her words leave me utterly confused.

"Oh, my god, you piece of shit. Why won't you stay? Honestly, how many pieces of tape is it going to take? This shouldn't be so hard."

But I'm even more confused when I walk into the kitchen and find her standing barefoot on top of my countertops. Between her teeth, she holds a roll of Scotch tape while her hands attempt to secure a long piece of black and white streamer to the top of the kitchen cabinet. Her pretty face brightens when it seems to finally stick, but before she can celebrate her victory, the other end of the streamer that is connected to the other side of the room comes undone.

"*Fuck*," she groans around the roll of tape as her head falls back in frustration.

By the looks of my kitchen, it appears she's succeeded in making other pieces of streamer stay in place at least a couple dozen times. Black and white decorations elaborately crisscross the entire span of the ceiling, and matching balloons are tied to each of the four barstools.

What the hell is going on in here?

"You were so close," I remark, finally stepping further into the room and announcing my presence.

Indie spins so fast in my direction, she nearly topples off the countertop. The way my heart seizes in my chest at the fear of her unintentionally hurting herself is painful and, frankly, *unexpected*. When did her safety and wellbeing become a true concern of mine? She isn't supposed to be more than a plaything. Right?

My legs have me darting toward her before my mind has a chance to catch up, but luckily for us both, she manages to regain her balance.

Her amber eyes dart to me and her mouth gapes, the roll of tape falling to the hardwood floors. "*Shit!* You're here already!"

Hands tucked casually into the pockets of my slacks, I take a few steps closer. "Yes, I'm here. Almost two hours later than expected because of the rain." You'd think in a state that rains as much as Washington, people would learn to fucking drive in it.

"*It's raining?*" Indie's head snaps in the direction of the large windows overlooking the back deck.

"Yes."

At neck-breaking speeds, Indie jumps from the countertop and sprints to the glass back doors. She disappears through them without an explanation or look back at me. Through the heavy rainfall, I hear sharp curses come from her.

A moment later, she reenters the house, white shirt and hair already damp with water. In her hand she holds the strings of a large bouquet of black and white balloons. Her eyes frantically look for a place to leave them before she gives up and just lets them go. They promptly float to the ceiling as she darts back out the open doors.

She returns again, this time with sopping wet streamers—the same ones decorating my kitchen—tangled around her arms and hands. The paper is practically disintegrating into nothing before our eyes, but she doesn't appear to be willing to give up on them yet. She dumps them on the kitchen island before attempting to go back outside for presumably more decorations.

My hand locks around her upper arm before she can run back into the rain.

"Indie." I attempt to pull her attention away from her frantic task, but she seems to be steadfast on her mission to save whatever remains outside because she pays me no mind. Her eyes barely flick in my direction. So, I try again, this time, with a sterner tone. "*Indie.* Stop."

"No!" she argues. "I was trying to make it special and now it's all getting *ruined.*"

I'm still so lost on what is happening here. "You were trying to make *what* special?"

She stops fighting me and I release her arm. The defeated look on her face reminds me of the one she wore when she first came to my office asking for help.

Indie pushes the wet strands of her hair off her forehead, and sighs, "Your birthday."

It's not often I'm completely caught off guard but right now, I am.

"*My birthday?*" I repeat, sounding as dumbfounded as I feel.

My obvious shock must be lost on her because she continues with her rattled and chaotic explanation.

"You've done so much to help me, and I wanted to return the favor, but I'm also a firm believer that everyone should have their birthday celebrated. I had this whole plan to surprise you when you got home, but it's not exactly going to plan ..." she trails off, eyes looking at the balloons that are now floating against my twelve-foot ceilings. "It was overcast, but still pretty nice out so I decorated the deck thinking it'd be fun to sit out there, but I finished early and my too-much gene kicked in and then I thought 'hey, why don't I decorate the kitchen too?'" Her face pinches in a grimace. "But that took longer than I expected, and I lost track of time, and now you're here and I look like a hot mess." Her fingers tug at the loose white T-shirt she wears with a pair of cotton shorts.

"But all of this? You did for me? For my birthday?" With a quick look at the balloon tied to the bar chairs, I find that they do in fact say *'Happy Birthday'* in a whimsical curly font.

Indie looks at me like I've grown a second head. "Yes, for *your* birthday. Come on, Astor, keep up with me here."

As my name falls from her lips, I realize it's the first time she's ever addressed me by name. It happens so casually and comfortably, it's as if she's been doing so for years. It's in this very moment that I discover that not only do I want her to address me as such moving forward, I also want to know what it's like to have her scream my name as I fuck her.

Like a little kid excited to show off a new toy, she dashes to the stainless-steel refrigerator and pulls out two pink boxes. Flipping the lids, she reveals two personal sized cakes.

"I didn't know if you were a chocolate or vanilla fan, so I got both to be safe." Before I have a chance to respond, she reaches into the freezer and pulls out a pint of ice cream. "If you're not a cake person, I also got ice cream. Again, I had to guess on the flavor. I guess if you want to be crazy, you can have both. I won't judge."

At this point, I find I'm truly too stunned to respond to anything she's saying. All I can do is stand here as she flits around me showing me what she's done. For *me*.

She picks up a perfectly wrapped present from the breakfast nook table. "This is from Callan. He said I could just leave it in the cardboard shipping box it came in, but that felt ... *wrong*. So, I wrapped it for him."

Callan. That explains how she knew it was my birthday. Up until she mentioned it, I myself had forgotten that it was today. It stopped being a noteworthy day for me long ago.

"Oh! I also got you candles, but I'm thinking you're not really a 'blow out candles and make a wish' kind of guy." Her frantic flurry comes to an end and as it does, her big amber eyes stare at me expectantly.

And as I stand there, staring blankly back at her, I watch the hope drain from her expression.

"This was a big mistake, wasn't it? Oh, fuck, you hate it. Callan said you didn't celebrate, and like an *idiot*, I never thought to ask why. Is all of this dredging up horrible traumatic childhood memories? *Shit, shit, shit.* Okay, here just ... look away and I'll take it all down."

With a new mission, she rushes past me and beelines for the very countertop she'd been standing on when I got home. She's just about climbed up when my arm loops around her thin waist and I hoist her away.

"What? No! Put me down so I can put all this crap away." When I ignore her request, she begins to struggle in my hold.

Wordlessly, I turn her in my hold and place her back on the countertop in a sitting position. Of course, she can't help but try to get away one last time, but my hands lock on her bare legs, trapping her in place. "Enough. Sit still."

"I'm so embarrassed. Just let me go, Astor." She sighs as she drops her face into her hands.

My finger lifts her chin up, forcing her to look at me. "Why are you embarrassed?"

Her eyebrows pull together. "Are you *seriously* asking me that right now?" Her hands gesture wildly around the decorated space. "Look around you! I did all of this for you, and not once did I ever consider that you may not like it."

As if on cue, one of the long pieces of streamer comes undone and the end of it flutters to the ground. At the sight, Indie's whole body slumps and a whimper comes from her frowning lips.

"Who says I don't like it?"

"Umm ... your *face* does? I may not know what type of cake you prefer or what your favorite color is—hence the black and white decorations—but I think by now I've learned to read your facial expressions."

She tries to pull away from me again, and this time I cup the side of her face, threading my fingers into her damp hair in the process. "Well, pretty girl, I hate to be the one to tell you this, but it seems you may need more practice, because you're wrong. I don't hate it." I'm not sure how I feel about it yet, but I know it's quite the opposite of hate. "You simply ... caught me off guard. Up until the very moment you said this was all for me—for my *birthday*—I hadn't realized it was today."

"What? How is that possible? You can't just *forget* your birthday."

"The last time I truly celebrated my birthday was when I was seventeen years old. When my mother passed the next year, my father declared we no longer needed to participate in such trivial things like birthdays or holidays. After that, those special days became just normal Tuesdays or Thursdays." I tried to go out of my way to do the opposite for Callan when he was a child, but I'll admit it didn't come easy. In many ways, I'm sure I've failed my son, and this was probably another example of my fatherly shortcomings.

Big amber eyes full of sorrow look up at me. "I'm sorry, Astor."

"It's okay. I never felt like I was missing out on anything special." I look around the room, examining all the effort she put into this for me. "Until now."

The light returns to her face as relief sets in her features. "Maybe you were just missing someone to celebrate with."

"Perhaps."

No part of our arrangement required she do something like this, and yet, she went out of her way to make today special for me. I can't remember a time that someone went through so much effort for me without it being demanded of them. She simply did this because she *wanted* to.

I find myself staring at her as if I'm suddenly seeing her in a brand-new light. Like the cloud of lust and uncontrollable hunger I've had for her is momentarily lifted, and I'm left seeing the kind-hearted and warm woman she is. There's some black smudged under her eyes from running out in the rain and her cheeks are flushed from the lingering embarrassment. Her hair is tangled and mussed from the wind and from having my fingers woven into the strands, but still, she looks beautiful staring up at me.

My prolonged examination of her has Indie's teeth nibbling

on her pink bottom lip. The action only amplifies my sudden desire to kiss her. When she smiles softly up at me and whispers, "Happy birthday, Astor," I give into the yearning.

At the first brush of my mouth against hers, it has her body seizing in shock and my breath locking painfully in my chest. I can't remember the last time I truly wanted to kiss a woman, but with Indie, I feel like if I don't kiss her now, I'll regret not doing so the rest of my life. I already have a long list of regrets, and this is one I don't want added to it.

As if we're both giving in to the moment—to each other—the caged air in my lungs finally releases and Indie melts into my touch. The victory I experience when she kisses me back is unexpected but somehow welcomed.

Her hands reach out for me, but at the first brush of her fingers against my button-down-clad shoulders, she retracts them like she's been caught doing something that isn't allowed. It dawns on me that, until this moment, she's never been the one to initiate touch. I've always been the one to reach for her first, so she simply doesn't know that she's *allowed* to return the favor.

It's my fault. I've never given her any reason to believe otherwise.

"Touch me," I growl against her soft lips.

With the unspoken restriction lifted, I learn that Indie has been holding back all this time. Her hands are everywhere and anywhere all at once, tracing every line of my chest and back as I devour her mouth. I lick along her seam, and she parts for me eagerly, sliding her tongue against mine. A delicious moan comes from her throat as her fingers venture to the short strands of my hair. She tugs at them, pulling me closer to her.

My cock, straining against my slacks, is eagerly waiting to be buried in her once more, but for now, I'm enjoying this. It's new and addicting in its own *refreshing* way. In the past, when I've kissed a woman like so, I've done so with the promise of it leading to the bedroom, but right now, I just want to experience this. I want to explore her and her sweet kisses for a while longer.

As I do so, I begin to wonder if this arrangement is somehow evolving past just sex? Is my plaything becoming a toy I want to keep? As she clings to my body, moaning, I begin to wonder if that's truly a bad thing.

NINETEEN
INDIE

I HOLD the phone closer to my ear as I step out of the busy coffee shop where I've been studying between classes. Tessa's talking to me, but her words stopped registering a minute ago when she broke the news. The tears of relief started welling in my eyes almost immediately, and now that I'm standing on the sidewalk alone, they're freely falling.

"Indie, did you hear what I said?" Tessa questions. "Another animal rights organization bought the entire lot of horses. A donor came through and they offered twice what we were able to. They've all been moved to a temporary horse sanctuary near Snohomish. Amy and I are headed there as we speak. If Jupiter is there like we think he is, he's safe, Indie."

"Really?" My voice is thick with overwhelming emotion, and my bottom lip wobbles as I fight a sob. I wipe the tears from my face, but it's no use. More fall seconds later. "He's safe."

"We have every reason to believe that he was there. Two people have reported seeing a horse that matches his description. They even talked about the white mark on his hind leg."

Doubt still creeps in like ice water crashing down on a happy moment. "They could be wrong. A black horse isn't exactly rare."

Tessa is quick to shut down my reservations though. "We're choosing to believe that it's him until we know otherwise."

"Okay." My head nods as I think over my next steps. There's only one thing I can do now, right? "Send me the address. I'm meeting you there. I need to see for myself if it's him." I'm already rushing back inside the shop and shoving everything into my bag, not caring if the notes I'd been working on for hours wrinkle or tear.

"I think you should stay put, Indie. Some of the horses are probably in rough shape and it can be grim. You shouldn't have to see it."

While I appreciate her looking out for me, I'm not taking her suggestion. "I said I'm coming. Text me the address, Tess." I disconnect the line before she has a chance to argue with me further.

The heels of my leather boots pound into the ground as I run out of the establishment and down the sidewalk to where I parked my car. My bag spills out everywhere on the passenger side floorboard when I toss it inside. That's a problem and a mess for another time. My focus is on Jupiter now. For two months I've been waiting for this phone call. The chances still aren't in my favor, but this is the closest we've ever gotten and I'm clinging to the sliver of hope that he's truly there waiting for me.

Before I back out of the parking spot I'm in, I decide to send Astor a quick text. He'll want to know where I am if I don't show up tonight like we'd planned. Since his birthday two weeks ago, we've had dinner together almost every night. I'm honestly not sure how it started, but without even trying, we've fallen into an easy routine. At night, one of us picks up food on our way home, and in the mornings, whoever is up first brings the other coffee. Within the first two days, he'd learned to make it just how I like it, though he relentlessly chastises me for the amount of sugar I use.

I'll admit it feels a little like we're playing house. I'm not complaining though. The shift between us since that night has been nice. *Really nice.* The intoxicating heat and passion between us hasn't simmered down, but there's now a comfortability between us that was lacking before. Like we've both slowly started shedding the walls we'd unknowingly put up.

At this point, the tricky part is not getting too comfortable. There's still an end date looming in our future. Just like my relationship with Callan, my arrangement with Astor is short term. Next spring, we'll have to go our separate ways, and already the very thought of doing so creates an unpleasant feeling in my chest. I'm quickly becoming attached.

Indie: I'll explain later, but I'll be home late. I'm sorry.

As my message sends to him, one from Tessa pops up with the address, and all thoughts of waiting for his reply disappear into thin air. I'm sure there will be hell to pay later with him, but any punishment I must endure at Astor's hands is worth it if I truly do get Jupiter back.

TRAILERS ARE SCATTERED ALL around the large piece of property and volunteers in matching light blue shirts are helping lead the rescued horses into the large barn-like structure in the middle. I wonder if the newly liberated animals know that they're safe now, that their value is no longer being measured by the amount of meat they can provide. Each one is getting a new lease on life, and I'm excited for each one of them even if I'm only here for one horse in particular.

With Tessa and Amy involved, I know they'll all go to homes they can thrive in. The couple won't adopt them out until they are one hundred percent sure they'll be safe in their new home. Knowing Tessa, she'd keep the whole herd herself if she needed to. If it came down to it, she has the resources and ability to do so.

Like she's been pacing the walls waiting for me to show up, Tessa appears in the wide doorway before I have a chance to enter the chaos happening inside. From the looks of it, there must be at least forty people here helping unload and separate the horses into stalls and various round pins.

Tessa's wild curly hair is tied into a bun on top of her head and her freckled face looks troubled when she steps in front of me. Her expression is usually one of positivity. She's definitely one of those obnoxious glass half full people. That's why, without her having to even say it aloud, I know.

"He's not here, is he?" I'm proud of how I'm able to keep my voice even and calm when I feel as if my soul is breaking in sharp, irreparable pieces. "He was never part of this group, was he? It was a different horse they saw."

Tessa's head shakes. "That's the thing, Indie. It *was* him. We were right, he *was* there."

My heart constricts painfully in my chest and dread snakes down my spine and limbs, a cold fog following in its wake. "What do you mean *was*? Where is he now? What happened to my horse, Tessa?" Calmness has abandoned me all together and panic has stepped up in its place.

My trainer's mouth opens and closes like she doesn't know how to find the words. What's happened that is so hard for her to say aloud? Flashes of every horrible possibility flip through my head in a frenzied storm.

"Is he dead?" I choke out, my throat and eyes burning.

This has her whole body jolting in surprise and her hands reach for my shoulders. "No, no, honey. He's not dead." Despite her reassuring words and the way she now holds me, it does little to soothe my fear.

My breath is coming in shaky gasps as I plead with her. "How do you know for a fact that he was here? Did you see him yourself? Please just tell me."

She reaches into the dark-red puffer vest she wears and hands me a polaroid photo. With trembling fingers, I take it from her and choke on a sob when I examine it. The picture is small and grainy, but his fear and malnutrition are crystal clear. The strong stallion that always stood so tall with confidence is nowhere to be seen. Jupiter is too skinny and the same look of defeat I've worn these last few months is evident in his posture. He looks like he's close to giving up.

"The organization that rescued them takes these of each of the horses and posts them on a bulletin board at their headquarters so they can remember who they're fighting for. This was taken earlier this morning when they first got to the auction lot," Tessa explains gently. "Rachel, the woman in charge of all of this, gave it to me when she explained what happened."

"If this was taken this morning, where is he now?"

She tucks the strand of hair that's fallen into my face behind my ear. The motion is so motherly, but it doesn't bring me any comfort. "He's already been adopted, Indie. The woman who donated the large sum of money to purchase all the horses had one stipulation. She wanted Jupiter. Rachel couldn't refuse her and risk the rest of the horses getting sent across the border. She had to give him to her."

Tears pour out of my eyes, landing on the photo in my hand. "Why him? Why'd she want Jupiter?"

Tessa's head shakes sorrowfully. "Rachel doesn't know. She tried to explain your situation, but the woman was determined to take him with her."

"So that's it? He really is gone now?"

"I think so, honey." I expect her to tell me she has a plan of action on how to get my horse back, but the fight in her is gone. She's accepted the situation. "But he's *safe*. This situation feels hopeless and I'm terribly sorry it didn't end how either one of us wanted, but I want you to remember that he's *alive*. That's what is important."

"I'm just supposed to, what, *give up*? Move on?" Just saying those words aloud was painful and difficult, how am I supposed to actually follow through with it?

"I don't really see another option, sweetheart."

I feel like I'm being buried alive with everything that's been thrown my way these past few months. The sliver of hope that in the end I'd win and get Jupiter back has kept my head above the surface. The fact that I have truly lost him has boney, cold fingers of defeat wrapping around my ankles and they're pulling me under.

In this moment of utter despair, I'm not even sure I care that I can't breathe.

TWENTY MINUTES.

That's how long I drove before the tears became too blinding and I had to pull to the side of the road. And here I've sat for two hours. The sun has gone down, and I think my phone died. The constant obnoxious buzzing of phone calls and texts stopped a while ago. Maybe Astor and Tessa just gave up and are letting me have the space I so desperately need right now.

I need time to mourn, and I don't think I'll be able to do that at Astor's house, let alone in front of him. Our walls are coming down, but I doubt dealing with my emotional breakdown is part of the arrangement Astor created or something he's prepared to do.

My tears stopped coming a little while ago. Even if I wanted to cry more, I think my tear ducts have temporarily gone on strike. So now I sit here in silence on this dark back country road waiting for the same acceptance Tessa found so easily to come to me, but it's not happening. No matter how hard I try, I can't see the positive angle.

I lost my best friend and last link to my dad today.

My dad. I wonder if he's disappointed in me that I couldn't find Jupiter in time. He's probably more upset that I allowed him to be taken in the first place. I'm pretty sure I'm disappointed enough in myself for the both of us.

Horribly bright headlights shine into my dark car as an SUV drives down the road. This happens every couple of minutes, and each time I just shield my sensitive, swollen eyes and wait for them to pass. This time is different though. They make an illegal U-turn right as they reach me.

Alarm bells go off in my head when they park right behind me. For the first time since I pulled over, the realization that I'm all alone in the middle of bumfuck nowhere with a dead cellphone hits me. This all but confirms I'd be the first one dead in a horror movie.

Frozen in fear for only a second, I jump into action. Turning the keys in the ignition, I prepare to drive away like a bat out of hell, but with one last look in my rearview mirror, my escape plan goes out the window. As it does, a different kind of fear settles in my bones.

I'm not about to be abducted. No, I'm about to be scolded.

Astor found me.

TWENTY
ASTOR

THE PLANS I'd made for tonight imploded when she'd sent me that text.

She said she was going to be late and so I waited an hour for her to finally come home, but she never did. Every single one of my phone calls and text messages went unanswered. Each time her sweet voice recited her voicemail message in my ear, my anger only grew. I'm not sure how many traffic laws I broke as I drove down here in a fury, but I'm lucky that I'm not currently being detained by police officers as we speak.

As I walk up to her car and finally lay my eyes on her, I come to the startling realization that the emotion I was feeling wasn't anger. It was distress. Besides my son, I can't remember a time I was this concerned over another's safety like I am with Indie's. Every possibility of what could have happened played in my head as I searched for her. For a minute, I even entertained the idea that she'd left me and her life here behind, but that idea was ultimately disregarded. She's worked too hard to remain here to walk away from it now.

Indie's friend, Tessa, had finally called my office and Cheska had given her my cell phone number. The trainer knew that Indie was staying with me and wanted to know if she'd made it home safe as she too had been trying to get ahold of Indie for some time. She'd explained that Indie had left in an emotional state after learning her beloved horse had already been adopted. Tessa graciously gave me the address of where the sanctuary was before we hung up and I used that as a starting point for my search to find my girl.

Indie doesn't turn her head when I stop beside her driver's side door. Her eyes stay stubbornly pointed ahead. It's not until my knuckles rap against the glass does she move, but even then, it's only to roll down her window.

Not really interested in exchanging pleasantries on the side of this goddamn road, I get straight to the point. "What the fuck do you think you're doing out here? What have I said about forcing me to search you out, Indie? I don't do *this*." And yet for her, I've done it twice. "Get out of the fucking car. We're leaving."

My nonnegotiable order has her hackles rising and head whipping in my direction. Fury blazes in her like amber fire. "Don't act like someone forced you to drive out here. I sure as shit didn't. All I needed was a little while to collect my thoughts —*to process*—what happened. I figured all your ignored calls would have conveyed that message clearly, but apparently you can't take a fucking hint, Mr. Banes."

My molars grind. She hasn't called me that since the night of my birthday, and right now, it feels like a slap in the face. "Have you forgotten who you're talking to?"

Now that she's finally looking at me and with the help of my car's bright headlights, I take stock of her appearance. Her eyeliner and mascara are smeared under her swollen, red eyes. God knows how long she sat here and cried. Her complexion is pale, and she just looks exhausted—emotionally and physically.

Her head shakes. "Nope, I know *exactly* who I'm talking to, and I hope that also makes it obvious just how serious I'm being when I tell you to leave. I can't do this with you right now. Losing Jupiter has taken *everything* out of me, I have nothing left to give you." She's trying to be strong, but I can hear the slight hitch in her voice as she fights the building sobs.

"As I recall, I haven't yet asked you to give me anything."

"Yeah? Well, the night is young. What happens when we go home and you want me to spread my legs for you? Am I just supposed to shove down the utter despair I'm feeling and do it happily with a smile on my face?"

She's projecting her anger at me. I'm well aware of this and can even say I understand it, but I can't stop the surge of rage in my veins. "You really think so lowly of me, Indie, that you think I'd ask you to fuck me while you have snot running down your face and tears in your eyes?"

Finding my question humorous, she chokes out a sardonic laugh. "Since when do you have to *ask*? Isn't that the deal we made? *'Mine to call upon, mine to have when I please, mine to touch in any way I see fit.'* That's what you said, isn't it?"

My fingers curl into angry fists, and to resist further denting her piece of shit car with them, I simply place them on top of the car and lean down so we're eye level. "This is your one pass, pretty girl. I'm going to forget you said that because I know you're heartbroken right now, but before we completely move on, I want to ask you one question. Can you name one occasion in which I've physically forced you to do something you didn't truly want to do? That you didn't fucking *crave*?"

She tries to keep up the fight, but within seconds it melts from her body and the flames extinguish in her big sad eyes. "No," she sighs. "You haven't forced me to do anything I didn't want to do."

"That's what I fucking thought," I growl in agreement. "Now, you have five seconds to get out of this car yourself. If you choose to continue to be stubborn, I will pull you through this fucking window."

Wordlessly, she rolls up the window and collects her things. A minute later, she emerges from the car looking thoroughly miserable and dejected.

"Let's go. We've wasted enough time out here as it is." The original plan I'd foreseen for tonight is ruined, but I still may be able to salvage some of it if we can get there before they close for the night.

"What about my car? What if someone steals it?"

I glance at the silver sedan that is probably just shy of two years older than her. The parts that it would take to get it in proper working order would be thousands of dollars more than it's worth. "Then they'd be doing you a fucking favor." Before she can argue with me, I take her bag from her and thread my fingers through hers. "Come on, pretty girl, let's get you home."

TWENTY-ONE
INDIE

IF MY GRIEF wasn't going to keep me quiet on the drive home, embarrassment for my behavior with Astor sure as hell is. The whole hour drive back home, I can't even bring myself to look at him or even out the window. Instead, I just stare at my lap and get lost in the memories I was fortunate enough to create with Jupiter and my dad. All of my best ones include one or both of them, and I think that's part of what makes this so hard. All I have left of either of them are memories.

My fear now is that I'm going to start to forget them. What will I do then? I don't have anyone in my life that I can reminisce about them with now that my mom has all but disowned me. I'm suddenly feeling very *alone* in this world. They've all left me, and each second that passes brings Astor one step closer to doing the same thing.

What a really fucking depressing thought.

I don't look up until Astor's Porsche SUV comes to a stop and his window rolls down. For a split second, I think he's stopped at a drive-thru, but the very thought of Astor Banes consuming fast food is laughable. His palate is far too refined for such a thing. I'm shocked to find that we've stopped in front of a large iron gate and that Astor is rolling down his window to a man sitting in the small security shack attached to it.

"Astor Banes," he tells the guard. "We were supposed to arrive earlier, but I called and warned we'd be late. The owner authorized it."

The guard shifts in his seat. "Ah, so you're the guy I'm getting paid overtime for."

Astor stares blankly at the man, not a single fuck reflected in his expression. Keeping the conversation short and to the point, he tersely responds with, "We'll be here for less than an hour."

"Fine by me, dude. I've got a kid starting college next year, I need all the overtime I can get." He shrugs before hitting a button that opens the metal gate.

Ignoring the man's waving hand, Astor rolls up the window and pulls through the gate. Thirty seconds later, the smooth asphalt street turns into rough gravel as we follow the single lane road illuminated by ornate streetlamps. Having completely checked out during our drive here, I have no sense of direction. It's so dark out here, I can't see any nearby landmarks to help with my bearings.

"Where are we?" I question him. "I just want to go home, Astor. It's been such a horrible day."

"This whole thing would be far less confusing for you had we come here in the daylight like I'd originally planned. Had you simply answered your phone or, better yet, come home like you were supposed to, you would understand."

My arms tighten across my chest as a scowl forms on my face. "You're not really going to sit here and scold me for attempting to find Jupiter, are you?"

He doesn't offer me a response; his eyes simply glance over at me. The expression on his face is truly unreadable and I'm still trying to decipher it as we come to a stop in front of a large building. No, not a building ... *a barn*.

"Why on earth would you bring me to a barn *today* of all days?"

Again, he ignores me. Cutting the engine, he gets out and walks around the car to open my door. In a move that seems too *gallant* for Astor, he offers his hand to help me out of the SUV. Suspicious and a little wounded he'd bring me here when my emotional cuts are still bleeding profusely, I hesitate a moment before reluctantly allowing him to lead me away from the car.

This barn is nothing like the one I was raised in or the one I'm currently working at. This one screams money and luxury. The exterior is made of pretty stone and cedar wood, both of which are visible because of the warm glow of the lanterns mounted about. The wrought iron that accents each of the arched windows completes the pretty aesthetic. I know without having seen any of the horses inside that they're worth more than most luxury vehicles, and the people that board them here are in similar tax brackets as Astor.

He procures a key card out of his jacket pocket and scans it on the fancy electronic lock. Why the fuck does Astor have a key to a *barn*? His thing is falconry, not horses. The light flashes green and he releases my hand to open the door for me.

Just like a moment ago, I pause before walking inside, and this only causes his eyes to roll and an exasperated sigh to escape him.

"Do you require an engraved invitation? Get inside." To ensure I do as I'm told, his free hand reaches for the small of my back and he gives me a slight push inside.

Just like the exterior, the interior is made of the same cedar wood and pretty iron finishes. There are even rustic looking chandeliers hanging from the two-story high ceiling. Meanwhile, at my current barn, the light in the tack room has been out for weeks. They keep saying they'll fix it, but as of two days ago, I'm still using my phone flashlight to find my supplies.

I stand there partially in awe of the place, just staring down the long row of stalls on either side of the barn. There must be at least thirty of them, and from the looks of it, they're mostly occupied with horses. I swallow hard when I feel the pain of my loss creep to the surface. In an attempt to not completely lose it in front of Astor, I clear my throat and turn around.

My chin drops to my chest and my eyes squeeze shut like it will somehow help block out my surroundings. "I don't want to be here," I whimper.

But, of course, he won't accept this. Astor's finger comes under my chin and forces me to look up at him. The tenderness I find in his stormy eyes makes my air catch. This side of him is completely new to me. The closest I've come to seeing this look is the night he kissed me for the first time, but even then, it didn't come close to this.

"You told me once that you whistled every time you entered a barn, why didn't you just now?"

I can't believe he remembers me telling him that. At the time, I wasn't even sure he was listening to me talk about the habit I picked up from my dad. "What's the point in doing so when I know that he's gone? When I know there won't be an answer?"

The corner of Astor's mouth lifts in a shadow of a smile. "Humor me."

My brows furrow as I frown up at him. "Is this some kind of sick game to you? If so, I'm not having fun, Astor."

He shakes his head at this. "Just do it, Indie."

Grudgingly, I lick my bottom lip and pull in a lung full of air. I grew up hearing this whistle, it doesn't matter how much time passes, it's a sound that I will always be able to recreate. I'm pretty sure I mastered it before I learned how to speak most words.

The sound echoes through the vast space and the hurt pieces of my soul. My heart breaks a little more when we're unsurprisingly met by deafening silence.

"See?" I sniff, tears welling in my eyes. "A totally pointless exercise—"

A noise I truly never thought I'd hear again has my entire world stopping and heart thudding painfully against my ribcage. The whinny is softer than usual, but still, I know it belongs to him. I'd recognize it anywhere. No matter how it might change or differ, I could still pick it out of a crowd of hundreds.

I'm unable to stop the choked sob from escaping. "He's here?"

Astor gently grasps either side of my face and his thumbs wipe away the cascade of tears. His next words are ones that I will cherish the rest of my life.

"He's here, baby."

TWENTY-TWO
ASTOR

THE CHOKED noise she makes sounds like one of pain as we reach his stall, but I know differently. It's one of complete and utter relief. This is the moment she's been fighting so hard for. The reunion that felt borderline impossible has finally come and the emotional event is enough to make Indie's stunningly beautiful face break into a million pieces at the sight of her beloved horse.

Indie's hands cover her face, and she unapologetically weeps into them. The sight makes an unreachable place in my sternum ache. Never in my forty-two years of life have I experienced such a sensation. Not until her. My Indie.

In a move that feels shockingly like second nature to me, like it's something I've always done, I reach out and pull her to me. She doesn't fight me, in fact, the second she makes contact with my chest, she melts into me. I hold her, hands soothing down her back, while she cries every last tear her body is capable of producing. I can't bring myself to care that her tears and makeup are staining my light gray dress shirt.

"It's okay, pretty girl, I've got you," I whisper my reassurance—*my promise*—to her.

For several minutes, we remain like this before she finally releases a shuddering breath and withdraws back. Red-rimmed amber eyes look up at me, a look of awe and gratitude shimmering brightly in them.

"You did this ..." Indie starts, voice scratchy from her emotional rollercoaster of a day. "You were the mystery donor that saved them all. You saved Jupiter."

Being praised for a good deed is something completely foreign to me. It creates an uneasy sensation to form under my skin. Yet another thing I'm not accustomed to. "I can't honestly say that purchasing the entire herd was part of my original plan. Jupiter was my main and only concern, but I couldn't very well leave them all there now, could I?"

I did it because I knew *she'd* want me to, and for some reason, that became my driving force. This whole relationship started with my desire to have *her* please *me*, and now, the roles have been reversed. *I* want to please *her*. I want to ease her constant and unrelenting worry. I want to be the reason she doesn't frown in her sleep any longer. Simply, I want to be the reason she smiles.

When it comes down to it, I suppose I can't say my motives were all selfless.

"But why did Tessa say a woman was behind all of this?"

"Her name is Giuliana. She's worked for my family for almost a decade now. They send her to handle business on their behalf when they can't or don't want to do it themselves. Occasionally, I still require her help, and since she has a bleeding heart much like you, she was more than happy to handle this for me." It was probably a nice break from her usual business dealings. Fuck knows the shit she's seen working under Emeric's control. "Once we had confirmation that Jupiter was in fact at that facility two weeks ago, we've been arranging his freedom ever since."

Indie's head shakes in disbelief at this. "I don't ... I don't understand. You really did all of this to free him?"

"No, I didn't do it for him," I admit, tucking the short strands of her dark hair behind her ear. "I did it for you, pretty girl."

In a matter of seconds, I think four different emotions cross her face as she processes my admission. "*Astor.*" My name on her lips sounds like the sweetest prayer my ears have ever heard. "I don't know how I'll be able to repay you for this. I don't know what else I have to offer you, but I'll find a way to make it up to you."

When I put my plans in motion to make Indie mine, I only saw a temporary arrangement in which I used her until I got my fill. I never could have foreseen that I'd end up here, doing something as big as this simply because I craved making her happy just as much as I craved her body. Maybe more.

My original plan has gone off the rails and I need to decide soon what I'm going to do moving forward. Do I lean into this new development, or do I retreat before we're both in too deep? The things I am wanting from her now are ones I've always claimed I didn't want from *anyone*, and I find that discovery alarming.

"I don't want anything in return this time," I promise her. "You've already given more than I ever expected from you." Her mouth opens like she wants to say more, but the horse moving in the stall drags her attention away from me and our conversation. Which is probably for the best.

Pulling away from me, Indie shifts toward the barred stall door. Her fingers tug at the sliding door lock warily. "I'm allowed to go in, right?"

"He's your horse, baby. You can do whatever you want, but please do be cautious. It took four people to get him into this stall and the vet had to administer a mild sedative when he examined him this afternoon."

"Did the vet clear him?"

"He's severely malnourished and desperately needs to put weight on, but he didn't find any physical injuries other than a few scrapes. Those probably came from fighting the handlers or other horses at the facility." Giuliana forwarded me pictures of what the inside of the auction house was like. In each holding stall or pen, there was anywhere from four to eight horses stuck inside. They were forced to stand the entire time as there was very little room to lie down. "They drew blood, and they'll check for any infections or diseases he may have picked up. We should get those in the next couple days. He recommended Jupiter remain quarantined away from other horses for a while just as a precaution."

The stallion's entire body jerks when Indie slowly slides the door open. "Hi, buddy," Indie greets. "I've missed you so damn much." She keeps her voice low and her movements slow as she inches toward him. His black ears perk up and the unease that's been in his dark eyes since we arrived lessens at the sight of his longtime companion. "I'm so sorry it took so long to get you back."

Jupiter shifts back a foot to create more distance between them, but unwilling to give up yet, Indie gently lifts her hand out to him. His nostrils flare as he breathes in her familiar scent and for a moment, I believe that he's going to come to her. That changes a split second later when the stallion's ears pin to his head and he rears up on his hind legs. In a flurry of hooves and angry noises, he lunges at her.

I reach for her just in time. If I'd acted even a second later, she would have been gravely injured because the furious horse comes down right where she'd been standing. Yanking Indie out of the stall and safely behind me, I slam the sliding door closed just as Jupiter charges toward us once more.

"Fuck," I mutter under my breath.

Indie's eyes flick between me and Jupiter, her expression completely horrified. "I knew he would need time to heal, but for some reason I didn't think it'd be this bad. He won't let me anywhere near him. He doesn't trust me anymore." The elation of their reunion is officially gone and concern forms in its place.

"He's traumatized. It's just going to take time." I try to reassure her even though my own doubt is running rampant. It's not an option, but the side of me fueled by my newfound desire to keep her safe demands that I order her to stay away from the animal. I know that wouldn't work because if someone asked that of me with my eagle, I'd fucking laugh in their face. "You held his trust once, Indie. You'll earn it again."

Her hand scrubs her pale face and she paces in front of me. The smeared makeup under her eyes can't even fully conceal the dark circles forming, but I wouldn't need those to tell me how tired she is. I can see it in her eyes, the vibrant energy that usually sits in them has dimmed. She needs rest.

"Let's get you home so I can put you to bed. You need to sleep off this day."

Immediately, her head is shaking and her chin is lifting in stubbornness. "No, not yet. I don't want to leave him."

"You can come back tomorrow or anytime you want. You have your own access codes and key cards waiting for you at home, but you need to sleep, and he needs time to acclimate to his new surroundings. Let him calm down some before you try to work with him again."

"Maybe we can stay just another hour," she tries to bargain, as if I'm someone who can be negotiated with. You'd think she'd understand that about me by now.

"I apologize if I gave you the impression that this was up for further discussion. So let me rephrase to clear up any confusion. We're going home so you can get some rest. You can either walk out of this barn on your own two feet, or I will carry you out. Either way, you're leaving right now."

She stands there like she's truly thinking over her options. Tired of waiting, I shift forward and prepare to haul her over my shoulder, but she retreats back multiple feet and holds her arm out like that will be enough to keep me at bay.

"Fine," Indie growls unhappily, the most adorable, pathetic scowl on her face. "You win."

"I always do."

TWENTY-THREE
ASTOR

SHE WASN'T at the house when I got home, which isn't surprising since every spare moment Indie now has in her already busy schedule is spent at the barn. It's been three weeks since Jupiter was returned to her, and for most of those days, I've come home to an empty house. You'd think after living alone for many years, I would be accustomed to the silence and solitude. Instead, I find myself yearning to hear the soft music she listens to when she studies or the sound of her laughing. The house is just too quiet when she's not there.

But mostly, I miss walking through the front door and being greeted with her smile. In my life, there've been very few people who are genuinely happy to see me enter a room. Indie is the exception. Even half asleep and exhausted, a small smile forms on her lips in the morning when she first rolls over and finds me there beside her.

When Indie moved into my house, my thought was that I'd be able to preserve my own space and she'd be granted hers. Sharing a bed with her never crossed my mind, but somewhere along the way, I stopped leaving her bedroom after I ravaged her body at night. This change happened all on its own and we've yet to acknowledge it. It's just another sign that I may be getting too close and accustomed to her presence.

I keep telling myself that I need to do better, that I need to resolidify our boundaries and stick to the original arrangement set forth between us, but then I go and do dumb shit like this.

Indie keeps her phone on silent here so the sound of it doesn't startle her still unstable and unpredictable thoroughbred. It's well past eleven at night and all my calls have gone unanswered. This is the latest she's ever stayed at the barn, and that, coupled with the fact we were supposed to have dinner together tonight, had me driving out here. I'm telling myself I'm only here because I want to check on her wellbeing, and not for the other slightly alarming reason—that I find myself craving her company.

Two weeks ago, she'd come home with cut-up hands and knees. Apparently, Jupiter had charged at her again and she'd fallen when she tried to get out of his way. Indie shrugged it off like it wasn't a big deal, but that didn't stop me from requesting she only work with the horse when someone else is present. These late nights when she's the only one at the barn leave her in a vulnerable position. If she were to get severely injured, it could be hours before someone found her.

In a fashion true to Indie, she completely disregarded my suggestion and said, "You're cute." Then she'd pressed a soft kiss on my mouth before leaving for the day.

Horses turn their heads to look at me as I pass by their stalls on my way to the very last one. The whole barn is quiet and there aren't any signs of Indie anywhere, but I know she's still here because the car I've loaned her is parked out front. I did eventually send someone back to collect hers, but after truly inspecting that shit-box, I decided she wasn't going to drive it any longer. Her dashboard lights up like Christmas day when she turns on the fucking thing, every sensor light shining bright.

Stopping at the stall, I observe the black horse inside. He's put on some weight already, but he still has a ways to go. His blood tests came back clean, and his scrapes have all scabbed over. It's his mental injuries that now need tending most.

Not finding her at his stall, I'm about to go search the arena and the tack room when her soft voice suddenly says my name.

"Astor?" It's barely a whisper and it takes me a minute to figure out it's indeed coming from inside the stall.

Keeping my eyes on the hostile horse, I tentatively open the sliding door and peek inside. Sure enough, Indie sits on the wood shaving-covered stall floor with her back pressed against the wall. Her head lolls in my direction and she gives me that smile I've been craving all day.

"Hi."

I stay where I am, not daring to move any closer to the pair. It'd only take one wrong move to spook the animal. "What the hell are you doing down there?"

"I'm making Jupiter get used to me again," she explains. "I'm hoping if I keep this up, he'll remember that I'm not a threat to him, and then he'll come to me. It's too much for him when I approach him, so I'm putting the ball in his court." She rests her head back against the stall wall with a groan. "And it's *so* fucking boring."

Her new tactic makes sense to me, but still I can't help asking, "How long have you been sitting there?"

Indie's shoulder shrug. "Not sure, I left my phone in my bag, but I do know that it's been long enough for my ass to go numb." She shifts in place, a grimace forming on her face.

"It's almost midnight, which means unless you plan on sleeping in wood shavings like some kind of barnyard animal, it's time for you to come home with me."

She looks at her horse for a second before sighing. "Yeah, you're probably right."

"I know I am."

Through all of this, Indie hasn't taken time off from teaching lessons, and just last week, she had her midterm tests. There're barely enough hours in the day for everything she's trying to accomplish, yet somehow, she's still managing to do it all. *Tenacious little thing, she is.*

With slow measured movements, Indie climbs up from the floor. Jupiter's dark, wary eyes watch her, and his body stiffens like he's prepared to act if she dares to come too close. She's putting on a brave front, but his new behavior is breaking her heart. I've offered to hire another trainer to help work with him, but Indie is determined to do it herself with the occasional help from Tessa. She doesn't trust anyone else around him and I can't say I blame her.

Closing the stall door behind her, she turns her attention to me.

"Hi," she greets again as if we hadn't already exchanged pleasantries, but I don't mind since this time she accompanies her greeting with a soft kiss.

"Hi," I respond, matching her low whisper as her arms loop around my neck in a loose embrace. Big amber eyes, the same color as my favorite scotch, examine my face. I'm not sure what she's looking for, but she seems to find it because she leans in and kisses me again.

What starts off as a tender greeting quickly morphs into something else entirely. It's not surprising since Indie Riverton seems to have that effect on me. My desire to have her—to take her until she calls my name and my name only—started the first night Callan introduced her to me. With one look, I knew I wanted to call her mine. That feeling has only amplified and grown since our arrangement started. I expected that it would start to diminish after a while, *especially* after she moved in with me. It is my experience that too much time spent with someone is the quickest way to grow tired of them. But that's not the case with Indie. What we have now, it still doesn't feel like *enough*.

My hands tighten on Indie's delicate curves when her lips

part for me and her tongue glides against mine. She clings to me, nails digging and scratching at my neck and shoulders as I devour her mouth. It only takes one needy moan from her to have my cock aching for her. I just had her pussy this morning, but the untamed need burning in my veins would make you think otherwise.

Like a man starved for her touch—her body—I hold the back of her thighs and lift her up to me. The heels of her leather riding boots dig into my lower back and the extra inches I've granted her allow her to thread her fingers through my hair. It's something I've learned she loves to do, and I find myself loving the slight pain when she tugs at the strands.

"I need you," she pleads against my lips. "Fuck me."

Moving us forward, I push her against the stone wall next to Jupiter's stall. Indie makes a small gasping sound when her back collides with the rough surface. Using the wall to support some of her weight and keep her in place, I release one of my hands from her thigh so I can collar her throat with it. When we first started all of this, this act would have had a startled look appearing on her face. Now, a devious smirk pulls on her swollen lips and heat flames bright in her eyes.

I've trained my pretty girl well. She now craves my rough touch.

I apply enough pressure to get my point across, but not enough to hinder her breathing. "You wouldn't be giving me demands now, would you, Indie?" I lean in close, running my nose along her jaw. "You must have confused our roles because that's not your job. It's *mine*. I'm the only one here giving the fucking orders."

"Then give me some," Indie growls in frustration. "Tell me what you want from me. I'll do whatever you ask as long as it ends with me coming on your cock."

In five seconds flat, an idea comes to me, and I know exactly what I want from her tonight. "Get in the car and drive straight home. I will meet you there shortly."

Confusion crosses her lust-filled features. "You want me to *leave*? You can't be serious."

"Aren't I always?" I nip at her frowning bottom lip. "When I get home, I want to find you naked and ready for me in my bed."

"In *your* bed?" I haven't yet granted her access to my domain, but I suddenly yearn to smell her sweet scent on my sheets.

"Yes. Now go." There're a few things I need before I join her, and luckily, I can find both of them in the tack room here. Everything else is already at home waiting for us.

TWENTY-FOUR
ASTOR

JUST LIKE I ASKED, I find Indie naked and lying across my bed on her stomach. The only light in the room comes from the cracked bathroom door and the blue light of the cell phone she's on. When her eyes flick up from the screen to find me standing in the doorway, the endearing way her feet had been swaying about come to a halt and the relaxed atmosphere around her evaporates into mist.

That's right, pretty girl, I'm coming for you.

Stalking into the room at an unhurried, leisurely pace, I reflect over one of our first real conversations. "I told you once that if you discovered what motivates a person, you could train them to do anything. Do you remember when I said that?"

With the faint light of her phone, I can see the way her lips part as she takes a small inhale. "I remember."

Pulling the blue and silver silk tie I found in my car out of my pocket, I twist it around my fingers. "Have you discovered what motivates you, Indie?"

"Yes," she breathes. "You."

Triumph. That's the sensation that rockets through my body and right to my hardening cock. Finally reaching the end of the bed, I reach out and caress her jaw with my thumb. "That's my good girl." Her eyes flutter closed and she leans into my touch, but I rip it away far too soon for her liking. The pout she wears almost disappears entirely when I order, "Rise up on your knees for me."

Tossing her phone to the side, she gladly does what she's asked. Nearly eye level now, I can't help leaning in for a brief but hungry kiss. Indie returns it with as much passion and enthusiasm. I don't believe either one of us is ready for it to be over when I pull away from her.

"Close your eyes."

She flinches when the silk first brushes against her face but relaxes a second later when she realizes what I'm doing.

"Have you ever been blindfolded before?" I ask once I'm done securing the tie over her eyes.

Her tongue sneaks out, wetting her bottom lip before she answers. "No."

My finger begins to trace a line from her chin down toward her belly button. Her body shivers and a cascade of goosebumps erupt over her soft skin. "Good. It's another one of your firsts that I get to claim as my own." It's as if I'm going down a list, marking each one off as I go and engraving the memory of *me* into her brain.

Indie's hips jerk forward when my fingers trail past her navel and languidly over her pussy seam. Her hands flex at her sides like she's fighting the temptation to reach for me and further urge me to *really* touch her. If she wants to touch me, now is her chance because soon she won't be able to. She won't be able to do much of anything once I get her into the position I want her in.

"Fuck," she groans when I tease her opening.

"If I push my finger into you right now, will you be wet for me?"

Her head nods jerkily.

I add another finger and recreate the same motion as before. "Do you promise?"

"God, *yes*," she hisses. "I'm always wet for you, Astor. You simply look in my direction and I want you."

She does precisely the same thing to me. Just a single thought of her can have blood rushing to my cock. It happens during board and dinner meetings, and for the rest of those monotonous gatherings I have to force myself to focus on the task at hand and not her.

My fingers push into her and are instantly coated in her wetness, just like I knew they'd be. "My girl is many things, but a liar isn't one." I pump them inside of her, making sure to curl them forward to hit that spot inside of her that makes her breath catch in her throat. Not able to resist any longer, her hands reach for me. Her nails dig into my forearm as she implores me to continue what I'm doing. "Sorry to disappoint you, but you're not getting off like this. I just need to get you desperately wet and needy for me."

She whimpers pathetically when I remove my fingers from her core.

"Taste how much your body wants me." I drag my wet fingers over her mouth, painting her lips with her own need. Not needing further prompting, her tongue sweeps out and laps it up. The sight almost makes me snap and throw my plan out the window. Turning her over and fucking her just like this would be fun but I have *so* much more in mind.

I kiss her hard, sucking the remaining taste of her off her tongue in the process. Her fingers cling to me and pull me to her so that her bare chest is firmly pressed against me. I indulge this a minute longer before breaking away from her once again.

"Astor, please." Her beg is a sweet symphony to my ears.

"I want you on your stomach facing the headboard," I instruct gruffly. Her hands inch up toward the blindfold. Before she can reach it, my hands ensnare her wrists and stop her. "That will be staying on until I say otherwise. Understand?"

She nods her head once.

"Good, now do as I say."

Without a word, Indie turns away from me and lies gingerly on her stomach. The sight of her perfect round ass has my palm itching to leave a mark there. She'd look so good walking around with a bright red print of my hand.

"Don't move," I warn darkly before leaving her there and walking into the hall where I left the items I stole from the barn. If anyone notices they're missing, they can send me a fucking bill for all I care. With those in hand, I stop at my dresser and remove the black box from the top drawer. It's a box she'd recognize if she were able to currently see.

Returning to Indie, her head turns in my direction as she follows the sound of my movements. Without even touching her, her breathing comes in short pants. The anticipation of what's to come has already affected the way she breathes, and that pleases me to no end.

My hands glide up the back of her smooth thighs and she jolts at my light touch. "Keep your head and arms on the bed but lift up onto your knees." Not only will she look stunning in this position, but it'll also grant me unencumbered access to *all* of her. And that's precisely what I want from her. I want everything Indie Riverton has to offer, and I'll take whatever might remain.

She does as she's told with her perfect ass now in the air for me, and I help widen her stance until she's right where I need her to be.

"Beautiful," I praise. "Absolutely beautiful."

My compliment is accompanied with my palm coming down on her ass cheek. It's not hard enough to cause unbearable pain, but it's enough for a perfect red outline of my hand to form. Tonight, I'm going to make her look like my own personal art piece, and that mark is just the beginning of my design.

Taking one of the pieces of rope I liberated from the barn, I walk to the right side of the bed and loop it around her wrist. "Tonight, you're going to be completely at my mercy," I warn, tightening the knot enough that she can't escape it but it also won't dig painfully into her delicate skin. "How does that sound to you? Do you want to be my plaything, Indie."

Her response comes in a breathy moan. "*Always.*"

Using the red rope to manipulate her position, I bring her arm backwards and tie the ends around her thigh. Satisfaction blooms at the sight. She won't be able to move her arms or her legs. She'll be forced to stay right how I want her. Moving to the other side of the bed, I repeat the process.

Standing behind her, I take in the view of her perfectly displayed cunt. The light from the bathroom and hallway cast just enough of a glow for me to see everything.

Testing out the restraints, I drag my fingers through her slick heat, stopping for only a second to circle her clit. Like I expected her to, her muscles fight the ropes as her body reacts to my touch. Her hands, desperate to grab onto something, yank helplessly against her thigh.

"You're not going anywhere until I'm fucking done with you, baby," I explain sinisterly. "Like I said, you're completely at my mercy. I'm going to do whatever the fuck I want to you and you're going to take it like the good girl you are."

She groans into the pristine white comforter beneath her.

I tease her opening, pushing just the tip of my finger inside before retracting again. "Words, Indie. I want to hear your words."

Indie inhales a shuddering breath. "You can do whatever you want. please, just touch me."

Giving her a little bit of reprieve, I sink two fingers into her aching pussy. Indie twists her head as much as she can, giving me a hindered view of her face. The satisfied smile she wears as I finger fuck her has my hardening cock twitching in my slacks.

"Whatever I want, you say? Okay, baby, let's play."

With restricted movements, she grinds against my fingers the best she can. The softest whimper-like moans come from her throat, each one fueling the fire blazing in my veins. The hold this woman has on me is unmatched. I'm not sure that I'll ever find someone who makes me burn like she does. And I'm not sure if I *want* to find someone else. No, I'm fairly certain I've met my match. Now I just need to decide what I'm going to do about it.

Wanting to send her over with my tongue, I drop to my knees behind her and bury my face in her cunt. At the first languid swipe of my tongue through her seam, her entire body jolts as if she'd been struck by lightning.

"Oh, fuck," she cries. "More, Astor. Please."

Her head twists and turns against the comforter, my unrelenting tongue causing an extreme case of restlessness. I have no doubt that if she were able to move more, that she'd be thrashing all over the bed.

"You're fucking delicious." I once vowed I was going to eat her whole, and I lick and bite at her like a starved man consuming a decadent meal.

A strangled sound erupts from her, bouncing off the walls and further feeding my famished beast as she comes on my tongue. As she shudders and shakes, riding wave after wave of bliss that rockets through her nerves, I don't let up. I lap at her pussy until her cries quiet, and all that remains are the soft spasms of her aftershock.

When her muscles relax and she sags the best she can into the bed, I drag my tongue up toward the virgin hole we've been preparing to take my cock. We've gradually increased the size of the plugs, and she's finally ready for me.

The relaxed state she was in just a second ago shifts and she jerks in surprise.

"You said I could do anything I wanted, and I want to fuck

this tight ass with my fat cock." Driving my point home, I drag my tongue over the ring of muscle once more before standing from my kneeling position.

Picking up the black box that holds the largest of the three plugs I've used on her, I take it out and grab the bottle of lube. Indie's gotten more relaxed about this than she was the first time she experienced it. I can tell by the way her muscles tighten and her breathing becomes ragged that the unknown still makes her timid, but my brave girl never backs down from a challenge.

The clear lube drips down the crack of her ass and I catch it before it dribbles on the bed. Swiping it up with my finger, I drag it over her tight hole and thoroughly coat it inside and out. The second her muscles loosen and my finger slips inside, she moans at the small invasion. The unknown may be unsettling, but it sure as fuck feels good.

I remove my fingers and replace it with the silver plug. She pants into the bed, her restrained hands twist at her sides as her fingers curl into fists.

"Breathe and let it in," I encourage, increasing the pressure as it reaches the widest point. After another second of resistance, the plug slips perfectly into place and she relaxes once more. My thumb pushes at the base, and she groans. "Such a good girl. You're going to take my cock so well, aren't you?"

"Oh, god. *Yes*."

Continuing to press on the plug, I bring my other hand down on her ass. Leaving a mark identical to the one on the other side. She hisses out a breath, but her lips pull in a delighted smile. "You like a little pain with your pleasure, pretty girl?"

"I think ..." Indie trails off like she's having trouble remembering her words. "I think I just like whatever you do to me."

My fingers curl around the other item I'd taken from the barn. I chose this riding crop because it has the smoothest leather and looked absolutely pristine, like it hadn't yet been used. Indie twitches, not expecting to feel the end of it run up her inner thigh.

"You like anything I do to you?" I repeat, moving the crop over her handprint-marked ass and then up her spine. "Let's test that theory, why don't we?"

The smack of the crop hitting her skin is glorious and the pink flush that forms on her flesh afterward is an addictive sight. But the real intoxicating part of it is the sound that comes from Indie. A cross between a cry and a deprived moan.

"What about this?" The crop comes down on her right ass cheek. I'm mindful to keep the pressure right. I want it to sting and enhance her pleasure, not to wound her or cause her true pain. "Do you like this? Do you want more?"

Smack!

"Yes. *More*," she cries, her back arching as far as her restraints will allow her.

"Okay, baby, I'll give you more." She's not expecting it and even if I'd warned her properly, I don't think anything could have prepared her for the sensation of the crop flicking across her clit.

"*Fuck!*" Indie all but screams.

I repeat the action and this time it causes her to fight her restraints. Her raised hips sway as if she can't decide if she wants to lean into the crop or shy away from it.

"Do you think you could come from this?" My sinister question is accompanied with another steady blow to her cunt. "Shall I continue so we can find out?"

Her reply isn't incoherent, it's an animalistic like mewl.

Alternating between lighter and harsher hits, the crop smacks up against her clit over and over again. I do this until her wetness is dripping down her inner thighs, and her head has thrashed about so much her blindfold has lifted to her forehead.

"Oh my god," she sobs, body shaking uncontrollably. "I'm … I'm going to come. *Astor*!"

Indie screams so loud as she comes, I'm thankful my neighbors aren't too close. No doubt the police would be called. Her body goes rigid, and she strains against the red rope tied around her wrists. While she withers and cries through her release, I hastily remove all articles of clothing so I can be deep inside of her as soon as possible.

She makes a choked sound when my fingers brush through her overly sensitive seam, wiping up her wetness in the process. Wrapping my hand around my aching cock, I stroke myself and spread her cream over the entire length. My teeth clench and my hips rock into my touch as I do. The sight of her tied up and screaming for me was nearly enough to send me over the edge.

Positioning myself behind her tied-up frame, I examine her face. Eyes now visible from the misplaced blindfold lock with mine. Exhaustion is already setting in them, but that simply won't do.

"I'm not done with you yet," I warn, the tip of my cock spearing through her drenched pussy lips. "Not even close, baby."

Her lips part in a silent cry as I plunge into her swollen cunt in one deep unforgiving thrust. My own breath is momentarily stolen from me as I'm overtaken by the feeling of being buried completely inside her. Her walls tighten like a vice around me, and for a second, I worry that I'm going to come right then and there.

Fingers digging into her hips, I regain my composure and control.

"So full," she groans into the bedding.

This is the first time I've fucked her while she wears the larger plug, and her pussy has never felt tighter. "I'm sure you fucking are," I grit between clenched teeth. "But you can take it."

"I can take it," she repeats, whether she's agreeing with me or simply reminding herself is unclear and unimportant.

My thrusts are brutal and unrelenting, but she never asks me to slow down or ease up. Her desperate cries and mewls of need only encourage me to maintain my pace. There's not a chance she won't be sore tomorrow from my rough treatment of her, but it'll be in the most delicious way. Her muscles will ache with the memory of me.

Writhing beneath me, her breaths become labored, and the walls of her cunt begin to flutter. She can come, but I want her to do it when I'm balls-deep in her ass.

The airy gasp when I remove the silver plug is a glorious sound, and I'm tempted to reinsert the plug just so I can force it out of her again.

"Who does this pussy belong to?" I grit out, slamming into her once more.

"You. Only you."

Withdrawing from her dripping cunt, I press the swollen head of my cock at her virgin hole. She's dangling so close to the edge that she doesn't squirm or tense up when I apply light pressure. Indie's ready for me. "And this tight ass? Who is this about to belong to?"

I push forward, invading her just an inch or so, but the move has her pulling in a rush of oxygen.

As she exhales, she gives me the answer I yearn to hear. "You, it'll belong to you."

My hand runs soothingly up her spine, her flesh is warm and covered in a thin layer of sweat. "Push out as I push in. You're going to take all of me."

She whimpers as I sink deeper into her, her hips instinctually trying to retreat from the overwhelming amount of pressure.

"Shh, baby," I whisper, ignoring the ill-advised impulse to ram completely inside her. "Relax for me, and let me in."

After a moment of calming breaths, Indie does as she's instructed. Her muscles stop fighting the intrusion and she pushes back into me.

"Fuck, I don't think I've ever seen anything hotter than this," I growl, eyes locked on the sight of my dick slowly disappearing into her ass. "You're doing so good, Indie. Taking my entire cock like this."

When I'm fully sheathed, we're both breathing hard and the blood flowing in my veins feels like it's boiling. The flames of need I carry for her are now as powerful as a forest wildfire.

I stay fully seated, allowing her to grow accustomed to my girth, and within a few minutes, she grows restless beneath me.

"Are you ready?"

Her head nods wildly. "Jesus, just fucking *move* already."

I can't help but chuckle at her small demand. "You're a little whore for my cock, aren't you, pretty girl."

A degrading term should have the opposite effect on someone. She should be offended, but instead she simply moans in agreement and tilts her hips back to meet my shallow thrusts.

Our slow measured movements slowly increase and grow as her body full adjusts to me. Soon, I'm withdrawing nearly all the way before plunging back inside. She squirms and strains against the ropes, trying desperately to find ways to further her pleasure. I don't even have to ask what it is that she needs.

Leaving one hand on her hip, I reach between our connected bodies with the other to find her clit. The second I begin massaging slow methodical circles, it's like she's taken over. Sounds that are comparable to sobs come from her lips and her hips do their best grind against my touch.

My own release is barreling toward me at an alarming rate. For the third time tonight, Indie's orgasm rips through her, and moments later, I follow her into euphoric oblivion, her ass milking every drop of cum out of me.

TWENTY-FIVE
ASTOR

IT WASN'T my plan to stop at the office on my way home from the dinner meeting, but Cheska, my assistant, called and reminded me of an important file I will need for tomorrow's early seminar. If it wasn't being hosted off campus, I wouldn't worry about grabbing it tonight. It's just one more thing delaying me from returning home.

Returning to *her*.

She has a late private lesson tonight with one of her young riders, but no doubt she's already home and waiting for my return. My cock stiffens in my slacks as ideas of what I'm going to do to her tonight consume my thoughts.

The elevator stops on my floor, and I step out. The only lights on are the emergency ones that always remain on, and there's not a single sound besides my footfalls as I walk down the hallway that leads to my large corner office.

My hand wraps around the keys in my pocket but stop when I find my door already open and light casting into the semi-dark hallway.

Where someone else might be concerned over such a sight, I only feel irritation. It's a fact well known by my colleagues that my office is not a place for them to venture into. Not even Cheska will enter my office without me present and she's been my assistant for the better part of five years. My own son won't do it as it's a lesson that's been ingrained in his brain since childhood.

Whoever has entered my office isn't afraid of my wrath, it would seem.

Teeth clenched, I push the door open wider and enter the lit office.

My annoyance only grows when I lock eyes with the person sitting in my chair with their feet on my desk.

"Mr. Blackwell—or is it Wilde now? I'm afraid I can't keep it straight since it keeps changing," I greet tightly. "Are you lost?"

The soft light of the phone he stares at illuminates his bitter grin. "Wilde is fine and nope. You're just the man I wanted to see." His cold blue eyes flick in my direction briefly before the device in his hand recaptures his attention. "A little birdy told me that you'd be stopping by tonight, so I thought I'd wait here for you to show up. Took you long enough. Naturally, I was so bored I had to poke around your files a little bit. Hope you don't mind."

"Naturally," I repeat, completely unamused. "Find anything interesting?"

He laughs darkly, a sound devoid of any true humor. "Nothing I didn't already know, but then again, there's not much I don't know. Is there?" Sighing, he stuffs the phone into the front pocket of his ripped and faded jeans. This kid has more money than most people will see in their lifetime, but he can't be bothered to purchase new jeans or tie the laces of his scuffed leather boots. "Though, I did learn something new last week that captured my interest."

"Is that so?" I lean against the doorjamb, arms crossing. "Who's the unlucky soul that traded you for this information?"

It's no secret to me what kind of business he runs. I allow

him to continue with his underground dealings on my campus with the understanding that if I'm ever in need of information, he'll give it to me free of charge. It's a deal that's worked well for me in the past.

His feet finally drop off my desk. He sits forward in my chair, arms resting on his knees, looking completely at ease in a space that isn't his to command.

"You really should vet your staff better, Banes. Could have protected yourself from something like this happening." Arrogance all but pours from his lips as he talks. "A redhead with an expensive nose candy habit came to me for a loan when she couldn't afford to pay her dealer. I offered a couple different payment plans to this ... *Chelsea?* ... bitch, but when she said she had some information about her boss, I was intrigued. And when she coughed up the information, I was fucking *ecstatic*."

Cheska? What the fuck does she know?

"What do you think you know, Wilde?"

"I don't *think* I know anything," he corrects. "You should know by now that when information is brought to me, I complete my due diligence and fact check the fuck out of it."

"Spit whatever the hell you have to say out, Rafferty. I have places to be and people I'd much rather spend my time with."

"Oh, I'm sure you do." He's a cocky son of a bitch, has been since he was in high school. He and Callan attended the same private school for a couple years when Rafferty transferred out right before his senior year. "A sweet little thing by the name of Indie Riverton, if I'm not mistaken."

The sound of Indie's name on his lips has my spine snapping straight and anger pooling in my stomach. "You have no idea what you're talking about."

His icy eyes meet mine, and as if we're having a battle of the wills, neither one of us looks away. Both of us waiting for the other to break.

After a minute, Rafferty's mouth pulls in a wicked smile, and he sits back in the leather rolling chair. "Here's the deal, Banes. I know about your dealings with Indie. I know what you did to keep her on this campus after she lost her scholarship and I know exactly what she's paying you in return. Like I said, you should really vet your staff. Your assistant is hot, but she's got a mouth on her the size of Texas and likes to listen to your private meetings through your door. Consider yourself lucky that *I'm* the one with this information. In the wrong hands, it could be really bad for you."

Still doubtful, I ask, "What kind of proof could you possibly have?"

"Well, there's the large sum of money you're paying your own college for her tuition," he shocks me by saying. "What? You thought by having the payment come from a bogus shell account that it couldn't be tracked back to you." His head cocks, dark brown hair falling on his forehead. "Does Indie know that you didn't actually get her scholarship back for her, or is that another one of your dirty little secrets?"

The strings that I could pull were just enough to keep her enrolled in Olympic Sound. There are strict rules regarding our merit scholarships, and once she had that mark on her record, there was no way she could become eligible for it again.

Grinding my teeth, I close the door before stalking across the room. "Cut to the chase, Rafferty. What do you want to make this information disappear?"

If it got out that I was involved in an intimate relationship with a student, it wouldn't be ideal, but it's a scandal I could easily overcome. It'd be even easier to do if there were plans to transition the relationship into a more serious and permanent arrangement like marriage. But if the unsavory details of our relationship were revealed, I'm not convinced that's something I could overcome without much difficulty. Coercing a student into a sexual arrangement in exchange for sexual favors isn't something people will willingly look past. My last name and social status couldn't protect me from that level of scrutiny.

"It's simple really." The Rafferty that I knew when he was in high school had a darkness around him, but at the time, there was still a glimmer of light in his eyes and smile. He had moments where he was happy. The Rafferty that sits in front of me now has fully succumbed to the pitch-black darkness. He's consumed by it and I'm not sure he remembers the meaning of the word happy. "In the coming months, a student by the name of Posie Davenport will be requesting to transfer here next year. I need you to ensure she's accepted and given a tuition rate so low she can't refuse the offer."

Posie Davenport.

I recognize the name immediately, but he knew I would.

My head shakes in disbelief at him. "After all these years, you still can't move on. You're still not at peace with what happened, are you?"

Rafferty stands from my desk and takes the time to push in the chair. His face is completely devoid of any emotion as he comes to a stop in front of me. "Whatever peace I had, she stole from me five years ago and now I intend to do the same to her." His hand claps down on my shoulder. "I'm going to *ruin* her, and unless you want word to get out about your *extracurriculars*, you're going to help me get her here."

TWENTY-SIX
INDIE

THE UNTHINKABLE IS HAPPENING. I'm falling for him. Hard. It's not a pretty and graceful fall either. I'm crashing and spinning out of control as I descend into the alluring depths of Astor Banes. The relationship that started off as nothing more than a tit-for-tat scenario is morphing into something I don't think I'll be able to let go of so easily.

Walking away from him and going on with my life like I haven't been fully consumed by him seems like an impossibility. It breaks my heart thinking that it'll be an easy task for Astor. He'll go on like I was never there. In the grand scheme of his existence, I'm sure my time with him was just a blip. And while I can't confirm if any of this is truthfully how he feels, he hasn't given me any indication to think otherwise.

I know the logistics of making us work are muddy and difficult, but I want to try. The problem now is I have no fucking clue how to have this conversation with Astor. How do I ask him for more when I'm not sure he has it in him to do so? What if this is it? What if he's not capable of committing to something more real or permanent? What if eight months is all I get with him?

The feel of Jupiter's lead rope in my hand takes me back to

that night two weeks ago when Astor tied me up and made me experience so many sensations. I thought I was going to dissolve into a pile of ash on his comforter. Countless memorable things occurred that night, but why is the fact that he insisted we sleep in his bed that night the one I'm clinging to?

Before then, I wasn't ever allowed in there and he only slept with me in the guest room. I haven't slept in my bed once since that night. He even moved my toiletries into his bathroom. The sensation of playing house is only growing by the day and so is my comfortability with it all. With him.

We've moved so far past causal sex, it's not even in our rearview mirror anymore. We're driving at top-speed toward something else entirely and I can't help but worry it's a ravine full of heartbreak.

Jupiter allows me to lead him back to his stall after I've spent the last hour lunging him in the round pen. I cried tears of joy last week when he allowed me to put a halter on him, and then I cried even harder when he let me lead him around the arena. We're slowly inching back to normalcy.

Tessa, who'd been here last week, hugged and cried with me when we had our massive breakthrough. She told me that my dad would be proud of me, which only made me cry harder. He spent years training this horse; I'm simply refreshing the things he instilled in Jupiter. Countless hours I sat and watched him work with his horses. I'm hoping that his methods somehow rubbed off on me and I can get Jupiter to the horse he once was. Back to the horse my father left to me.

Tessa asked when I thought I'd be able to get Jupiter back to jumping, and I kind of laughed at that. Getting back into events is the last thing on my mind. All I want right now is for my horse to trust me and for the trauma clouding him to ease up. He needs time to heal, and I'll give him as much time as he needs. If he's never ready to compete again, I'll be fine with that.

Once in the stall, I reach up for the leather halter he wears.

Astor surprised me one morning with the brand-new tack. He'd left the expensive gifts in the kitchen for me to find, and when I'd tried to thank him for it, he'd acted so casually about the whole thing. He'd waved me off like it was nothing.

My lips twitch at the engraved gold nameplate on the halter. It proves that it wasn't nothing. If it wasn't a big deal, he wouldn't have gone through the trouble of engraving Jupiter's name on it.

My heart lurches in my throat when Jupiter's head lowers to help me reach the halter. It was something he'd always innately done but hasn't once since he's been back. Everyday we're making progress and I couldn't ask for more.

"Good boy," I praise softly, fingers brushing against the side of his neck. "You're doing so good. Thank you for not giving up on me entirely."

Wanting to reward him for his bravery today during our lessons, I turn to leave the stall to grab a handful of alfalfa pellets from the bag outside the door. I thought I'd kept my movements slow and steady enough to not spook him, but the second my back is to him Jupiter's entire demeanor changes. His front hoof paws at the floor and angry breaths repeatedly come from him.

"Whoa, buddy." Turning back to him, I try to soothe him, but my efforts only make it worse. His rises on his hind legs and flails his front legs about. In the past, I've immediately left his stall and allowed him his space. He's done so well the past week or so that I decide to see what happens if I stick around.

Arms raised and voice soft, I inch closer to the agitated animal. "Shh, Jupiter. It's okay. You're okay."

He crashes back to the ground in front of me with a furious whinny. What's confusing is he's not paying me any attention. Whatever has set him off this time isn't me as his focus is on something else entirely.

"What is it?" Curious, I begin to turn around to search for the source of his distress, but I never get the chance to discover what it is because from the corner of my eye I see something barreling toward my head. There isn't enough time to duck out of the way or cry out. The blow to the side of my head almost instantly steals my ability to stay standing and my vision darkens. I don't feel myself land on the wood shaving-covered floor, but a second later when my vision clears, I find myself looking up at Jupiter.

My lips part to yell for help, but I can't force myself to form a single word. Now that I think about it, I'm not sure if I even remember *how* to speak. My vision tilts and no matter how much my eyes blink in an effort to clear it, it continues to get worse. I'm going to pass out. The cold, numb-like sensation is slowly working its way through my body, and I know once it's thoroughly spread, I'll be met with darkness.

Oh my god, somebody help me.

The last thing I hear before I succumb to the serene nothingness are the sounds of Jupiter's distress and footsteps retreating.

TWENTY-SEVEN
ASTOR

THE PRESTIGIOUS BUSINESSMAN sitting across from me donated enough money last year for there to be a complete overhaul of the Performing Arts Department. That is the only reason I'm still sitting across from him, pretending I give a shit about his wife's short career on Broadway. I've politely nodded along, milking the one scotch I allow myself at these monotonous dinner meetings. It's meetings like these, the ones where I have to schmooze and rub elbows with people so they'll continue to donate to my school, that make me question how I'm not a raging alcoholic. With a bit more booze, I might actually find these people the slightest bit interesting.

I'd much rather be at home with Indie. At least the things that come out of her mouth can hold my attention. And frankly, she's my favorite person to be around. Everyone else pales in comparison to my girl.

Indie knew I had this meeting tonight and planned on staying late at the barn. She's kept me updated with the progress she's made with Jupiter and I'm exceedingly proud of her. Her dedication to that horse is unmatched.

My cell buzzes in the pocket of my black sports coat and I

briefly cut in on the mind-numbingly boring story. "Excuse me."

Looking down, I hope to see her name lit up across my screen, but instead I find Callan's. He was in New York again earlier this week, but I believe he's back now. We'd talked briefly about getting together for dinner or a drink. Knowing he'll understand that I can't talk right now, I reject his call and reluctantly return my attention to the man across the table from me.

"Sorry about that. Please continue." *And hurry the fuck up with this story.*

Not needing to be asked twice apparently, he does just that. "She was the understudy in that production, but unfortunately she never got to take the stage as the lead."

Oh, for fuck's sake. She was only an understudy? Why are we still having this conversation?

"Truly unfortunate indeed," I contribute politely, taking another pull of my scotch.

Continuing with his *charming* tale, my phone buzzes once more in my pocket. I nod along, pretending to listen as I check the device. Callan. *Again.* He never calls me like this. Even when he was fourteen years old and was left home alone for the first time, he didn't call me this much.

A shiver of alarm snakes down my spine.

"I do apologize, but I need to take this. It's my son." I don't wait for my dinner companion to answer before I excuse myself from the table and walk toward the front doors of the restaurant.

"Callan?" I question, accepting the call once I step outside.

"Dad!" One word, one syllable, that's all it takes for me to know something is terribly wrong. "Dad! Can you hear me? The reception is horrible in this place."

"I can hear you. What happened?"

A fear like I've never known seizes my chest at his next sentence. Before he's even finished explaining, I'm running toward the parking garage where I left my car. All concern and thoughts for my dinner meeting leave me instantly. I'll call the restaurant later and pay the bill.

"It's Indie. She's been hurt," my son explains in a rush. "Someone found her in a barn unconscious." He goes on to explain that it's some kind of head injury and that she's still not responsive, but I'm not really listening anymore. A coldness is working its way through my veins and a humming has started in my ears. "Where is she? What hospital was she taken to?" When he doesn't answer fast enough for my liking, I impatiently snap his name. "Callan! Fucking answer me."

THE AUTOMATIC GLASS DOORS OPEN, and I'm instantly greeted by the cold air conditioning and the scent of antiseptic. I broke every traffic law that exists on the way here, and honestly, I'm lucky that no one was hurt by my reckless driving. The poor valet outside the hospital barely had time to catch my keys when I tossed them at him before rushing inside.

Not feeling overly inclined to wait patiently, I push past the loitering people by the front desk. The woman in pale pink scrubs glowers at me as my palms come down harshly on the desk she sits at.

"Sir, you'll need to wait your—"

"Indie Riverton," I bark, cutting the woman off. "She was brought in with a head injury. I need to know where she is."

A hand touches my shoulder, and a voice comes from behind me. "Hey buddy, in case you missed it, there's a line here."

My fingers lock around the stranger's wrist. In one second, I've turned to face him and I'm twisting his arm violently in the wrong direction. "I don't give a fuck about some line." I have two rules; I don't search people out and I don't wait in lines.

"And you should think twice about laying your hands on people you don't know. You truly never know what someone is capable of doing."

For fifteen years, I've been removed from the family and the teachings that were instilled in me. I was taught to act first—usually violently—and deal with the fallout afterward. It's taken me a long time to learn how to thoroughly think over and be meticulous with my actions. These days, I plan everything down to the last variable.

But apparently all it takes for me to revert to my old ways is being kept from Indie. Getting blood on my hands once more doesn't seem so bad if it means that I'm reunited with her.

"Dad," Callan's voice echoes through the vast hospital waiting area and has me automatically releasing the patron in my grasp. Leaving him and the godforsaken line behind me, I stalk in the direction of my son and the nurse that walks with him.

"Where is she?" I question before either one of them has a chance to attempt polite pleasantries or greetings. "What's her status?" Pausing, I stare at my son. "And why were *you* called?"

Callan's broad shoulders shrug. "I guess Indie put me down as her emergency contact when she registered for fall classes. Which makes sense since she didn't really have anyone else in her life she could have added. They saw her student ID in her wallet when they searched it in the ambulance. They called the school, and it was my number they had on file. She probably forgot to change it after we broke up."

What he's saying makes sense, though I can't help but be agitated that I wasn't called. *Why would she add you as a contact, Astor? It's not as if you're in a real relationship. On paper, you're nothing more than Indie's roommate.* The unwanted thought has me scrubbing a hand over my jaw as regret settles in my bones.

"You didn't answer me before. How is she?" I ask, dropping my hand back to my side.

Callan's blue eyes, ones that look so much like his mother's at times, slide to the grandmotherly woman at his side. "They won't tell me anything other than what I told you on the phone. They're saying since she's still unconscious and can't consent to more information being shared, they can't disclose more."

"You understand we have to protect our patient's privacy." The nurse adds in, voice dripping with practiced politeness. "And there's the matter of you not being family."

"She doesn't *have* any family." I don't know why it only dawns on me right here and now how truly alone Indie is. Her mother has completely abandoned her in this world and has morphed into an enemy. All she has left is Jupiter and ... *me*. "She only has me, and I want to see her. Right *fucking* now."

I'm long past caring if Callan knows the truth and I don't bother mincing my words in front of him. This isn't the ideal way for him to find out what's been going on under my roof, but my priority right now is *her*. She's the injured one. I can deal with the consequences of my actions with Callan at a later time.

The woman bristles. "Sir, if you could refrain from using such language. This is a place of healing." Her small, beady eyes dart around our surroundings and to the waiting patients. "I'm sorry I can't offer you more. We will have to wait for Miss Riverton to regain consciousness and go from there."

Her answer is completely unacceptable to me. I'm this close to blowing past her and searching for Indie room by room when an alternative idea comes to me. "I need to see Elijah Hill right now."

"The general surgeon?" she questions, brows raising.

He's also a hospital board member. We've crossed paths many times at functions and fundraisers. He became a donor for Olympic Sound when his daughter Zadie was accepted last fall. It's moments like these that I realize just how valuable those boring dinners truly are.

"Yes. Page him immediately."

TWENTY-EIGHT
ASTOR

FIFTEEN MINUTES LATER, I'm getting exactly what I want. Elijah pulled the necessary strings, and he's now leading me and Callan up to her room in the neurology department. The same nurse has accompanied us the entire way and her disapproving look isn't having the effect she thinks it is. If she's trying to *shame* me or make me feel guilty for abusing my privileges, I'm afraid she's wasting her time. I will not feel guilt or shame, not when it's granted me access to Indie.

It's as if I won't be able to breathe property until I lay my own eyes on her.

Elijah stops at an open hospital room door and gestures his hand at it. "After you, Mr. Banes."

Not needing to be told twice, I march through the door. I thought seeing her would help me breathe, but seeing her slight frame in a hospital bed, connected to machines and IVs, only causes my chest to tighten exponentially more.

Her skin is pale, and bruising has already started to form around her eyes from the injury to her head. Clear tubing sits under her nose, supplementing her with additional oxygen. It's a relief to see they didn't have to intubate her.

"Whatever hit her in the head caused a brain bleed," Elijah explains, having looked over her file on his iPad on the way up here. She's not his patient nor is the brain his specialty, but he insisted on being the one to walk me through what's happened. I'm not overly picky about who gives me the information as long as *someone* does. "They suspect she'd been injured an hour prior to when she was found in the horse stall."

She was alone and hurt for over an hour? My god.

"The horse stall?" I repeat.

He looks at the nurse for confirmation, and at her slight nod, he reiterates the findings. "The working theory right now is the horse acted out and she simply got in its way. The first responders who were called had trouble working around the distressed animal. One of the paramedics nearly got kicked in the abdomen."

The visual of Jupiter rearing back and front legs flailing about that night in the barn comes to mind. "This was my fear. I *told* her this could happen." I barely recognize my own voice, there's an unease to it I haven't heard since my mother was dying. "What's the plan now? Do we just wait to see if the bleed heals on its own?"

"They've taken her for a CT scan, and the bleeding is minimal enough for now that they've elected to wait on surgery. They've administered medications to help with the swelling and now we just wait to see if those work. If the blood doesn't clear on its own, they will need to operate to drain it."

"Jesus," Callan breathes out next to me.

"All things considered, she's lucky. The bleeding could be much worse, but many patients in her condition just need the meds and to be monitored. They usually make full recoveries."

My head nods once in understanding before I return my attention to the unconscious woman in the bed. I'm disappointed in myself. Disappointed that I didn't push her harder to stay away from that dangerous horse and disappointed that it's taken something as drastic as this for me to fully realize what Indie means to me. I'm not ready to let her go.

"Alright, just talk to the nurses at the desk if you need me for any reason," Elijah offers before leaving the room.

I move closer to the side of the bed while Callan asks the nurse, "Are we allowed to stay in here?"

"Seeing as you've already gone over my head once, it seems fairly pointless telling you no again, doesn't it?"

Callan's eyes slide over the woman, the unimpressed look that all Banes men master before the age of five on his face. "I'm glad to see we're finally on the same page."

With an unamused scoff, the nurse stomps out the door.

My muscles feel uneasy as I lower myself into the chair next to the bed. If it weren't for the beeping heart monitor or tubing connected to her, she'd look just like she does in the morning when I wake up beside her. That peaceful, calming air still surrounds her now, but it's doing little to soothe my own agony.

Not caring if Callan sees me do it, I take her small pale hand in mine. Her fingers are icy compared to my heated skin. "She's freezing," I comment aloud. "We need to get her another blanket or turn up the heat in here."

"Okay," Callan agrees, voice low. "I'll go let someone know." He makes his way toward the closed door and pauses with his hand on the door handle. "Hey, Dad?"

"Yes?" My eyes flick in his direction and I find a serious look on his face.

"It's going to be okay. *She's* going to be okay." A small reassuring smile pulls on the corner of his lips. "You both will."

All I can think as he leaves the room is, *God, I fucking hope so.*

AN HOUR LATER, I sit in the same place staring at her pretty face while silently pleading for her to wake up. Callan has stayed with me even though I've told him he can leave and I'd call him with any updates, but he insists on being here for me. He stepped out of the room about five minutes ago to find us coffee that doesn't come out of a vending machine. He mentioned something about snacks too, but I'm the farthest thing from hungry.

Leaning forward, I brush the short strands of her hair off her face. "I need you to wake up, pretty girl," my voice is just barely an audible murmur. "I need to see those eyes of yours again. I just need ..." I trail off, head shaking. "Fuck, Indie, I just need you."

With my elbows on the edge of the bed, I close my eyes and rest my forehead against my clasped hands. It's taking everything in me to not get up and pace the short length of this room. But I refuse to get up from this chair unless I have to. I want to be right here and the first thing she sees when she wakes up.

I don't know how long I sit like this with thoughts of what our lives will look like moving forward swirling in my head. One thing is certain, our arrangement will need to be abolished. It was based solely on sex and greed, and those two things are no longer the driving forces for my affection toward her. I've evolved so far past that.

The question now is, without the arrangement in place, will she choose to stay?

Moving forward, there won't be any coercion or manipulation forcing her here. If she wants to remain with me, it must be her choice this time. And if she elects to leave, I will need to find a way to let her, even when every fiber of my being is screaming at me to find a way to permanently tether her to me.

Cold fingertips tracing down my forearm pull me away from my thoughts and have my head lifting. My eyes instantly clash with a pair of bright amber ones, and in a second, a thousand pounds of relief crash down on me.

"Astor."

My name on her lips is a soft, breathy whisper, but it will forever be my most treasured sound. It'll repeat in my head for many years to come.

"Pretty girl." I intertwine my fingers through hers and hold on for dear life. "There you are. I've been waiting for you."

Her lips pull in a smile and she instantly winces. "My ... head."

My head turns toward the exit, hoping I'll see a nurse or someone walk by the door Callan left open when he left. "I know, baby. We've got you, though. Don't worry."

She tries to nod in understanding, but the movement instantly causes her pain.

"Try not to move," I urge, cupping her face as gently as I can. Not listening to my warning, she turns her head into my touch like she's seeking out any source of comfort.

Big tears well in her eyes as she stares at me. "I'm really glad you're here with me."

"Where else would I possibly be? There isn't a single place I'd rather be than right here with you." It's amazing how easy it is to speak the truth once you finally accept it.

"Really?" she whispers hoarsely.

"Really." I bring the hand I hold up and kiss it softly. "Nothing could have kept me away." The blood I was willing to spill to get to her is evidence of that.

The tears run down Indie's face freely now. "Astor—" Her lips remain parted like she's going to add more, but she's suddenly overtaken by something completely out of our control. Her eyes, which had been so clear and awake seconds ago, roll into the back of her head as convulsions violently take over her small body. The monitors connected to her sound as her heart rate spikes and her oxygen levels drop.

She's not breathing.

She's not fucking breathing!

"Indie!" Flying into a standing position, I yell loud enough for someone to hear me through the open door. "We need help in here! She's seizing!"

I'm helpless to do anything but watch her shake and spasm uncontrollably in the bed. It's hard to ignore the desire to reach for her and hold her steady. I know doing so could cause further damage though.

Twenty seconds later, a team of people dressed in scrubs and white coats rush into the room. My world quiets as a powerless feeling creeps in like a thick, suffocating fog. People are yelling and someone shoves me backward when I don't move away fast enough.

"You need to leave so we can stabilize her," someone says, but it's like they're talking to me through a tunnel. "Sir!" they snap, loud enough to pull me out of my daze. "Leave the room immediately and wait outside."

Absolutely not. "I'm not leaving her."

The doctor's face hardens, and her voice rises. "This isn't up for discussion. Leave the room or I will have security remove you from the building completely!"

Fingers threading through the strands of my hair, I look one last time at Indie. The thought of leaving her alone makes my sternum ache but I have no choice. Walking away and out of the room might be one of the hardest things I've ever had to do.

The door closes behind me, effectively separating me from her. Even with the blood rushing in my ears, the hallway is too quiet compared to the chaos of her hospital room. Not knowing what else to do, I slide down the wall right outside her door and hold my head in my hands.

How is this happening?

"Dad?" Callan's voice cuts through the humming impairing my hearing. "Dad? What happened?"

My throat feels tight, and I'm forced to swallow the emotion down before I can answer him. "She started seizing ..." I trail off, clearing my throat again. "I don't know … I don't know what else is happening. They made me leave her. She's all alone in there."

Callan places the two paper travel cups of coffee on the nurse's station before easing himself on the ground next to me. Wordlessly, he reaches for me and gives my forearm a comforting squeeze. "They've got her. She's going to be okay."

"She has to be," I grunt, scrubbing my face like I can wash away the devastating feeling consuming me.

"She's far too stubborn and strong to give up that easily. You're not going to lose her, Dad," Callan says, catching me off guard. There's no judgment in his voice, only acceptance and understanding. "*Well,* not today anyway. You're kind of a dick, so she might get sick of your shit and run for the hills eventually, but today? She's not going anywhere."

Turning my head, I stare at my son. Sometimes I find myself shocked that he truly is a man now. The young boy I've raised for over twenty years has grown up. "How long have you known, Callan?"

He smiles at this. "You might recall me telling you that you don't give me enough credit." It was the night that he and Indie ended things officially. I hadn't understood what he meant then. "Dad, you're really good at hiding behind that passive mask of yours, but do you truly think I didn't see the way you looked at her? I knew the first night I brought Indie home that you wanted her. When I knew I couldn't use her any longer to get over Ophelia, I started bringing her to the lake."

"So, you purposely put her in my path?"

"Yep." He nods cockily. "And let's be real, you gave yourself away when you had her move into the house. You've never liked any of my girlfriends enough to have them live under your roof, and you're definitely *not* that generous."

For a full minute I'm too stunned to speak. Not once did he hint or give anything away that showed he played a role in all of this, and I can't help but feel proud of him that he was able to keep such a thing from me. He might just survive working with Emeric after all.

"You're really okay with this?" I ask him.

"Yeah, Dad. I'm okay with it," he promises. "Indie once said that all she wanted was for me to be happy. I want the same for her *and* for you. If you guys make each other happy, who the hell am I to stand in the way of that?"

I always said that I didn't care what Callan or anyone thought of what I was doing with Indie, but getting his blessing brings about a level of relief I didn't know I needed.

"She does make me happy." She makes me smile and feel lighter than I have in my entire life.

Leaning his head against the wall, he turns to me, blue eyes inquisitive. "Do you love her?"

How can I admit that to him when I haven't had a chance to tell her first? Instead, I simply say, "I just need her to be okay."

TWENTY-NINE
INDIE

MY ENTIRE BODY feels like it was run over by a bus, and then, just for good measure, they backed up and ran over my head again. Muscles I didn't even know I had are sore, and not the good kind of sore that Astor usually leaves me in. Despite all the pain and stiffness in my body, the only thing I can focus on is how damn thirsty I am. I feel like I've been snacking on cotton balls like it was my fucking job.

My heavy eyelids crack open, and the morning sun coming through the window instantly makes my retinas sting. Who left the curtains open? I always close them, afraid some perv might be looking at me at night.

Stifling a groan, I close my eyes again and turn my head away from the bright light.

Wait a second... The sun is up and it's morning.

What the hell? I don't remember going to bed last night. Out of habit, I reach my hand out and search for Astor. He's always here when I wake up, but my fingers don't brush against his warm skin like they usually do. No, they're met with something made of hard plastic.

Forcing my eyes open, I squint against the sun and look

around the room. *Nope*, this definitely isn't my room or Astor's. An obnoxious beeping sound I'd recognize anywhere comes from above my head. Lifting my head in its direction, I examine the steady green line of my heartbeat rising and falling on the screen, along with my other vitals.

Holy shit! I'm in the hospital.

In a completely clumsy manner, I pull myself into a sitting position, ignoring the way my body aches in protest. The IV pulls painfully in my arm when the tubing catches on the side of the hospital bed, and I carefully adjust it to allow more mobility.

I'm trying to remember what happened and how I ended up here. It's not until my eyes land on a sleeping Astor that it all comes back to me. His handsome face is like a key unlocking all the memories that had been momentarily stolen from me.

He lies back on a recliner-like chair across the room. His arms are crossed over his chest and his head rests against the back. His mouth is pulled in a frown and his shoulders twitch, making me worry he's having a bad dream. The dress shirt he wears is rolled up at the elbows and the first two buttons are undone, but that's not what really gets my attention. It's the fact that it's severely wrinkled. Astor Banes doesn't wear wrinkled or stained clothes.

Oh my god, he slept here.

The same sensation that took me over when I woke up the first time and saw him hits me at full force, nearly knocking the wind out of me. It's a combination of relief and intoxicating contentment. The fact that he was here both times I woke only makes my forbidden feelings for Astor multiply at an alarming rate. I'm in *so* much trouble when it comes to him.

Like he can feel my eyes on him in his sleep, his gray eyes open and lock with mine. He stares at me like he's not fully registering what he's seeing.

Needing to break the tense staring contest, I quip playfully, "Be honest, do I look as bad as I feel. Like on a scale from one to something that lives under a bridge, how bad is it?" I remember something slamming against my head and then losing consciousness multiple times. The notion that I may have needed surgery crosses my mind. "Oh my god, did they shave my head?"

I don't think I'd be sitting up in bed if I had brain surgery, but I could just be on *really* good drugs, right?

Astor stares at me for another second, face completely void of any emotion before a huge exhale of breath releases from his lungs. He leans forward in his chair, dropping his head into his hands. The lighthearted teasing vibe I was going for evaporates into thin air as I watch him shake his head slightly.

"Astor?" I try, eyebrows pulling together. "Please say something."

His head lifts, and he looks back at me. The dark circles and exhaustion on his face mirror how tired I feel.

"You scared the shit out of me, baby."

Scared of what I might find, my hand lightly touches the side of my head that pounds with each beat of my heart. I'm relieved when I find that I do in fact still have hair.

"But I'm okay, *right*?"

With a sigh, he stands from the chair and makes his way to me. Taking my face gently between his hands, Astor places a kiss on my forehead. I don't miss the way he inhales, like he's committing my scent to memory.

"Yeah, pretty girl, you're going to be okay. They got you on meds to reduce the swelling and once they added the anticonvulsive, the seizure stopped. You'll have to be monitored closely and go in for repeat scans to make sure the brain bleed has healed on its own."

A brain bleed? Jesus Christ.

I scoot over in the bed, trying to make as much room for him as possible in such a narrow space. He hesitates a second before sitting down next to me. He wraps his arm gingerly around my shoulders, and the ache in my muscles eases when I lean into him.

"I had a seizure?" I whisper, picking at the piece of tape holding my IV in place. At least the seizure explains why my whole body is sore and not just my head. "I just remember you being there talking to me and then ... *nothing.*"

He's quiet for a moment, his fingers tracing slow circles at the top of my arm. "I'm thankful that one of us doesn't have to remember that," he admits, voice gruff. "Do you remember the barn? Do you remember Jupiter hurting you?"

I jerk back so hard at his question that lightning-like pain shoots through me. "What?" I choke. "What do you mean *Jupiter* hurt me?"

Astor's face grows angry, fury marring his handsome features. "He didn't just hurt you, Indie. He could have *killed* you. That horse has been through too much. You've tried to help him heal, but I think it's time we consider bringing in someone else to work with him. It's more than you can handle."

I gape at him, equal parts confused and pissed at what he's saying. "What the fuck are you talking about, Astor?" My question has his eyebrows shooting toward his hairline. "Jupiter didn't do *this*!"

"They found you unconscious in his stall," he tries to explain, but I won't hear it.

"Yeah! Because that's where I was *attacked.*"

His body goes rigid, a dark look creeping across his face. "What are you saying?"

I shift in bed so I can see him better. "I'm saying how dare you blame Jupiter for this when someone else was there. They spooked him and when I turned around to see who it was, something slammed against my head. I heard their footsteps before I passed out."

"You hit your head very hard. Your memory isn't—"

I cut him off with a frustrated sound. "No, Astor! I remember this. See if they have security videos or something because I remember everything that happened at the barn. I remember almost everything from last night. Hell, I even remember seeing you when I woke up before and how fucking scared I was."

That's all it takes for the stiffness to leave him and his features to soften. "You had every reason to be scared. Waking up after being unconscious and not knowing where you are is jarring."

My eyes burn and my throat tightens as I shake my head at this. "That wasn't why I was scared. I was afraid of how relieved and happy I was to see you when I opened my eyes."

His hand reaches out and he cups my face, his thumb tracing my jaw. "Why would that scare you, baby?"

"Because you're here and you're mine now, but when our deal ends, I'm going to be left with nothing, and I'm going to wake up alone. It scares me how much it's going to hurt when that happens, and I'm afraid of how hard it's going to be for me to walk away from you when this is over."

"Indie…"

This isn't the ideal time or place to have this conversation, but I worry if I don't say it now, I won't ever find the courage again. "I think … I think if there's no real future for us and we still have an expiration date, you need to let me go now. If I stay until the end, I'm just going to fall deeper in love with you and then I really won't be able to recover when you leave me." His soft caress stills against my wobbling jaw. "It will *break* me, Astor." His name sounds like a hoarse cry on my lips.

Tears finally fall from my eyes and his fingers catch each one and he wipes them away. "I told you that your tears would be mine," he murmurs as he watches them trickle down. "And I want them to belong to me for much longer than eight months, pretty girl. Last night … was possibly one of the worst nights of my life. The prospect of losing you was *unbearable*. I don't think I've ever felt so hopeless." His words have a way of creating the best kind of pain in my heart. It's like they're permanently engraving themselves there. "I promised myself last night that if you wanted to leave, I'd have to find a way to let you go, but I don't think I can do it."

"You can't?"

"No, I can't. If you try, I will hunt you down and find another way to make you mine." That dark ominous smirk of his that makes my toes curl and insides warm grows on his face. "And this time I will make it permanent and then there will be no escaping me. You know how vast my resources are. There is nowhere on this planet you could hide where I couldn't find you. So, tell me, pretty girl, do you want to try and run from me?

"No," I murmur, the intensity of his words and gaze stealing my breath. "I don't want to go anywhere."

This isn't how I foresaw our arrangement going, but I honestly can't think of a better outcome. All it took for me to get everything I didn't know I wanted was a sinister deal with a god amongst men. And I'd do it all over again if it brought me here to this exact moment.

Astor's head tilts toward mine and his lips skim across mine. "Pity, I think I would have enjoyed hunting you."

THIRTY
ASTOR

SHE WAS RIGHT, someone else was at the barn three nights ago. They tried their best to keep their face away from the cameras, but they failed when they fled from the barn with the metal pipe still in their hand.

One of the reasons I chose that barn was for the intense level of security they promised me. Unfortunately for them, it seems they couldn't keep their word because someone made it all the way past the security points and was able to severely injure my girl.

They don't know it yet, but I'm about to wreak havoc on them and their business. The owners have apologized profusely and were generous enough to share the video feeds from that night. Sadly, for them, their good gestures won't be enough to save them from me and my wrath.

I've already made plans to relocate Jupiter to a different, more secure, location. Discussions with the property's owners about further advancing their security have already started, and I feel confident it will be a better fit. In the future, I might consider purchasing property with enough land for Jupiter and Periphas, but for now, this will do.

My lawyers and I will deal with the shortcomings of the current barn soon, until then, I need to handle the real perpetrator.

Sitting back in my desk chair, I watch the video again. The same level of fury I felt watching it for the first time an hour ago returns in full force. They thought they could get to her because she was all alone and had no one to protect her.

They were wrong though. Indie Riverton is *mine* and anyone who dares lay a hand on her subsequently signs their death warrant.

Selecting a number I haven't called in ages, I place my phone to my ear and wait for him to answer.

I can practically hear the grin in his voice when he picks up. "Well, isn't this a nice surprise?" Emeric greets. "What can I do for you, brother?"

While I mastered the art of hiding behind polite words and diplomacy like my father before me, my little brother has mastered the ability of making each syllable he speaks sound like a threat. He doesn't try to hide what he's capable of or who he is. He wears it proudly. I'm sure he finds freedom in doing so.

"I need you in Seattle. Now," I order, eyes still locked on the screen in front of me. "There's someone I need help taking care of."

Emeric cackles. "After all this time, you call me for a *favor*?"

"Yes," I bite out between clenched teeth. "I need this dealt with immediately and with as much discretion as possible. And unless you've truly lost your mind, I believe that is something you're capable of doing."

"Don't you worry a second about my mind, Astor. It's as clear and stable as it's always been." Emeric's patronizing tone makes my eyes roll in my head. He may be leading the family empire now, but he's still my baby brother. "What do you say we have my new protégé take care of your little problem. Might be a nice initiation for him, don't you think?"

"Callan isn't taking part in any of this, nor shall he ever know about it. Do you understand me?"

"Fine," he huffs, annoyed I'm ruining his fun. "So, what? You want me to fly across the country to dirty my hands so you don't have to? That doesn't exactly seem fair now, does it?"

"Who said anything about my hands staying clean?"

"Are you saying the great Astor Banes is ready to bloody his hands again?"

Violent and graphic memories of my life before this crash into me. Things I've done and haven't thought about in decades play in my head like a movie. And yet, it's still not enough to stop me from saying, "For her, I am."

"So, this is for a *lady*, then? Well slap my ass and color me surprised. My big brother is pussy whipped." Emeric's joyous, borderline manic, laugh fills my ears. "I can't wait to meet her. She must be special if she has you calling *me* for help."

"Are you going to come or not?" I question impatiently, ignoring his comment about Indie being special. I'll do everything in my power to keep them separated for as long as possible.

"Yeah, yeah. I'll be there. As a matter of fact, I'm already on my way to the airstrip." The private jet will get him here before nightfall. Perfect. "Are you going to tell me who the unlucky fucker is?"

A menacing grin pulls on my lips as the person in the security footage turns his head. "Ivan. His name is Ivan." I click on the other clip that I received from a local detective and ally. The traffic camera catches the car that Ivan had escaped to after he assaulted Indie run a red light. It also captures the person in the driver's seat. "And his wife."

COLD AIR FILLS the helicopter as Emeric slides the side door open. The sudden rush of wind and temperature change has our guests lifting their heads and eyes groggily opening. The drugs that were administered over two hours ago keep their focuses fuzzy and their movements sluggish. Leaving them perfectly vulnerable and malleable.

Holding onto the safety handle above the open door, Emeric leans dangerously far outside the helicopter and lets out a cheer loud enough to be heard over the whirling of the blades.

Indie's traitorous bitch mother and Ivan look at him and then frantically back to me.

I relax back in my seat across from them and cross my ankle over my knee. "Oh, don't worry. No one can hear him. We're fairly far from civilization," I explain loudly so they can hear me. "We're flying over the wilderness between the state line and Canada. So, as you can imagine, there's no one around to hear or see us up here for damn near forty miles."

With a joyous smirk on his face, Emeric returns to his seat next to me. His dark, almost black hair is sticking up all over the place from the wind, and his eyes that look much like mine shine with excitement. "Meaning, we can do whatever the fuck we want with you, and no one will be the wiser."

We're ghosts up here in the midnight sky. We've taken the necessary precautions to ensure that our flight plans are nonexistent, and our aircraft can't be picked up by any radar. The pilot is the same one who flies the private jet and he's worked for us for years. He's well compensated to keep his mouth shut and knows what will happen if he were to ever speak out against the Banes family.

"What is the meaning of this!" Ivan screams, his body fighting against the rope restraints that ensnare him. "Do you know who I am?"

I bark a laugh at this. "I know who you are, but do you know who *I* am?" I question, voice eerily calm and even.

This whole thing has been like riding a bicycle. The man I thought I left behind long ago has returned with little to no effort. Stepping back into his shoes was as easy as breathing.

"Why the fuck would I know who you—"

The mother nudges her elbow the best she can into his side, the rope around her wrists hindering her flexibility. "Ivan. It's *him*." Unlike Ivan, she's failing to keep the panic from her tone. Her terror is on full display, and I fear I might get drunk off it.

Ivan looks confused by her words for a second. His head turns back toward me, and as if he's finally taking the time to pay attention to who's sitting across from him, his face pales as recollection sets in.

"That's right," I nod in pity. "I'm assuming you've just put together how truly and utterly fucked you are."

Ivan, trying to regain his composure and hide his nerves, laughs at me, but the sound is forced and fake. "This is because of *her*? You're doing all of this because of my whore stepdaughter you've shacked up with?"

I can't help but growl at his usage of the term *'stepdaughter'*. Neither one of them should be allowed to call her their daughter. They forfeited that right months ago.

"Careful now," Emeric *tsks* next to me. "I'd watch that mouth of yours if I were you. We still have plenty of fuel. If you keep it up, we can fly around up here while I rip your teeth from your skull one by one. If I'm feeling arts and crafty, I can make a necklace out of them and send it to your mother for her birthday. Now wouldn't that be a lovely surprise for her?"

Indie's mother chokes on a sob, her face deathly pale. "Why are you doing this? It's between my daughter and us. It's a family matter. It does not concern you."

I fly forward in my seat, arms resting on my knees as I bite out, "That's where you're fucking wrong. When you abandoned your daughter, she became *mine*. You then attempted to try and *take* what is *mine*. Luckily you failed." The security video proved that Jupiter was innocent in all of this. When Ivan swung the pipe at Indie, Jupiter lunged at him and obstructed Ivan's movements. If he hadn't done so, the blow to Indie's head would have been fatal. Jupiter returned the favor and saved Indie's life. The two really are quite the pair. "As you can see, it *does* concern me. It concerns me a great deal and that is why I have gladly stepped in to take care of the problem."

"If you want to waste your time with that lying cunt, then by all means, have at it," Ivan seethes.

"That's why you did this? Because she's a *liar*?" I question, not understanding what he thinks she could have possibly lied about.

"First, she tried to interfere with my relationship with her mother by lying about those fucking cameras she found in her room, and then she and that bitch trainer of hers posted online about their *miracle reunion* with that goddamn horse."

"That horse belonged to me, and I could do whatever the hell I wanted with it," the mother jumps in, yelling in defense of her new husband. "How dare Tessa and Indie spread all those lies about us on the internet! How were we to know that he'd end up at a kill buyer?"

I hadn't known until recently that Tessa had shared Jupiter's story on her nonprofit's website. She didn't include either Ivan or the mother's name, but people were still able to link Jupiter back to them.

"I'm guessing you're regretting ever putting your name on his registration, aren't you?" I ask her mother. "Made it really easy for the animal right's activists to track you down and reveal what you did to that animal."

Ivan rocks forward in his seat harshly. If he wasn't tied at the wrists and ankles, he probably would have come at me just now. "They sent the article to my investors. They believed the lies and ended our business dealings. Apparently, they're a bunch of fucking *PETA* supporters. I've lost millions of dollars in deals because of that selfish bitch. She had to pay for what she did to me."

"There you go again with the name calling," Emeric sighs. "I was really hoping we could avoid the whole *teeth* thing. Mouths bleed so much, and I really don't want it on my clothes, dude."

Standing from my seat, I yank Ivan up by the wrinkled collar of his shirt. He sways on his feet, but my grip keeps him from falling over and out the open door.

"That's the truly funny thing in all of this. Indie has no idea that Tessa posted that article." My guess is Tessa snapped a picture of the reunited pair when she was there helping retrain Jupiter. "The only thing Indie is guilty of in all of this is believing her mother still cared for her, but you've both made it very clear that isn't the case."

"Indie was always a selfish brat. Her weak father always placated her," the woman yells at me, her shrill voice cutting through the *whooshing* of the helicopter sounds. "She should have just let that dumb fucking horse go, but no, she had to continue to be meddlesome."

Ivan rears back and spits at me, his saliva hitting my cheek. "She got what she deserved. My only regret is I didn't swing harder."

Wiping my face off on my shoulder, I grin at him, teeth grinding painfully. "And I think you're getting off too easy."

Before he can retort with another unsavory remark, I push him from the open door. His screams as he barrels toward the forest floor below are drowned out by the wind and helicopter blades, but his wife's are nearly loud enough to pierce my eardrums.

My only disappointment is I can't hear the sound of his body hitting the ground. The snapping of his bones would have been glorious.

"Ivan!" the mother screeches. "What did you do?"

Standing in front of her, I roughly grab hold of her chin and force her to look at me. "The chances of someone finding him at all are minimal, but the chances of them finding his body before it's nothing but broken bones are nonexistent. The wildlife is going to pick apart his flesh until there's nothing left." I meant it when I said we were in the middle of fucking nowhere. "You're lucky that you're not joining him down there."

"I'm not?" she sobs.

"No, at the end of the day, you're Indie's mother and I can't very well kill you." Which is truly unfortunate because I would really like to. "So, you'll go with my brother. I told him he can do whatever he likes with you as long as you continue to breathe. Though, I can bet whatever his plans may be, they're going to make you wish I'd let you join your husband."

"You're sick!"

Patting her cheek patronizingly, I say, "I know, but your daughter loves it."

Moving away from her, she breaks down into uncontrollable ugly sobs. The kind where there's an ungodly amount of spit and snot cascading down her face.

Closing the helicopter door, I pound on the cockpit door, signaling for the pilot to take us back to the remote field where we left the cars. The sun will be up by the time I return to Indie, but I'll be returning to her knowing that I've taken care of any threats to her. The medication she's still on makes her tired, and with any luck, she won't know I left her at the house under Callan's watchful eye. My son knew something was going on when I left, but he's still in the dark about his uncle being involved. It's my hope it stays that way.

Sitting back down in my seat next to Emeric, he turns to me with a wicked grin on his face. "That was brilliant, it's like you never left to become a stuffy academic." With a long, exaggerated sigh, he quickly adds, "My dick is rock hard right now."

Only my perverted brother would find what just happened *hot*.

Shaking my head, I just say, "Let's go home."

THIRTY-ONE
INDIE

I STARE at the detective standing in front of me and shrug my shoulders. "I'm sorry, sir, I haven't seen or talked to my mother since September. She got remarried and cut off all ties she had to me." Admitting that doesn't hurt like it probably should. Each day that passes without seeing or talking to her solidifies how much better off I am without her.

He writes something down on the notepad in his hand before asking, "What about the husband? Have you heard from him?"

Ivan's missing too? "Nope. We never saw eye to eye or got along. There isn't a single reason for me to talk to Ivan, or for him to reach out to me."

In actuality, I'm kind of terrified that if I were put in the same room as Ivan again, I'd try to claw his eyes out with my nails. And I'm far too cute to go to prison for assault.

This whole thing is sitting weird in my gut. The endless possibilities of what may have happened to them swirl in my brain as I give my statement to the officer. There's one likelihood in particular that seems the most probable and it's taking everything in me to keep my expression passive. If my suspicion is true, the last thing I want to do is let on to the detective that I know something.

"You're more than welcome to look through my phone if you'd like. You'd see the last phone call I received from my mother was when she evicted me from my apartment."

"Did her doing that make you hold a grudge?"

You can't be serious. They think I had something to do with them disappearing off the face of the planet?

I gesture around at the expansive lake house I now call home. "I think it's safe to say that I came out on top, don't you think?" Not to mention she played a massive role in placing Astor in my life. "If anything, I should be thanking her."

He scribbles something else on his pad before nodding his head, dismissing me. "Alright, Miss Riverton. We'll be in contact if we learn anything about your mother's whereabouts."

Walking across the foyer to the front door, I open it for him. "I appreciate it, but that's really not necessary. You can let me know if or when you find her, but otherwise I don't need updates."

"Your fallout with her must have been massive," he remarks, stopping in front of the open door.

"Just because you share blood with someone doesn't mean you have to love or even like them." If I've learned anything, it's that family doesn't have to be blood related. They're the people that show up for you when you need them and stand in your corner regardless. I now know what it's like to have that.

"I suppose you're right." His beady eyes scrutinize my face for a second, making him hesitate to walk through the door. "Are you sure you're okay, miss?"

The bruising around my eyes has started to turn a hideous green color and my dirty as hell hair is tied into two knots on my head. In other words, I can understand where his concern is coming from. "I'm fine. I had an accident at a barn."

After hearing my story about someone hitting me over the

head and my steadfast belief that Jupiter is innocent, Astor assured me that he'd investigate it himself before bothering the authorities. Which is another reason I think I know what happened to my mother and Ivan.

The man nods before finally walking down the front steps of the house.

I stand there for a second, watching his black and white SUV pull out of the long driveway before shutting the door and going in search of Astor. He mentioned something about working with Periphas before dinner, so I decide to start my search in the backyard.

HE STANDS in front of the grand aviary watching the golden eagle inside when I walk around the side of the house. Hearing me approach, his head turns in my direction, and a frown instantly forms on his handsome face.

"You're not supposed to be out of bed."

I'm still technically on bedrest from my accident. I was released from the hospital six days ago, and one of the conditions of my discharge was that I take it easy for the next two weeks.

For the most part, that's been easy to do since the intense headaches I'm still getting have forced me to stay in Astor's bed. The good news though is the last CT scan I got showed the bleeding has already started to subside. The doctors are hopeful I'll be symptom free in the next month or so.

Lucky is an understatement when it comes to all of this.

"I would be, except the doorbell kept ringing and I had to answer the door," I explain, pulling the soft white robe I wear tighter around me. The chill in the air makes goosebumps erupt over my skin. I guess I should have changed out of my cotton pajama shorts before coming out here.

Astor's brows raise. "Who was here?"

"A detective," I say pointedly. "Apparently, my mom and Ivan are missing. He wanted to know if I've seen them."

The mask that I recognize all too well falls firmly into place. "That's truly unfortunate."

My eyes narrow at him and his apathetic response. "What did you do?"

"Who says I did anything?"

Taking a step forward, I shift toward his tense frame. "Because I *know* you, Astor."

Now close enough for him to touch, he reaches for me and trails his fingers down the side of my face. "Then you know I'd never let anything happen to you." His gray eyes flick to the injured side of my head. "You think I'd allow him to live after he nearly killed you?"

Oh, fuck.

Five minutes ago, I was imagining myself being sent to prison for assaulting Ivan and now I'm picturing Astor wearing an orange jumpsuit for the rest of his life as he serves time for first degree murder.

What's equal parts troubling and funny is I'm not even surprised that Ivan was the one at the barn. Who else hates me enough to do something like that? Jupiter's reaction also makes more sense. Ivan was probably the last person he saw before he was sent into that hellhole.

"*Jesus Christ!*" I gape, shaky hand covering my mouth. "What were you thinking? What if this gets traced back to you? Then what are we going to do?" Oh my god, am I going to have to talk to him through a piece of bulletproof glass? "I want it noted for the record that I'm vehemently against conjugal visits. I'm usually down for anything when it comes to you, but that is where I draw the fucking line."

An unimpressed look appears on his face. "You seem to be forgetting who the hell I am and who my family is, Indie.

I'm not going to fucking prison. I'm not going *anywhere*, in fact."

Backing up, I hold my throbbing head between my hands. "Is my mom alive?" Even as I ask, I'm not sure if I really care. In my mind, the mother I once knew died when my father did. I've mourned her already. The woman who's been hellbent on ruining my life and hurting me is not worth my tears.

"She is," he tells me stiffly. "I've sent her off with Emeric. He'll deal with her, and you'll never have to see her again."

Hearing this news, there should be a vast array of emotions wreaking havoc through me, but they're nowhere to be found. All I feel is indifference for the fact she's been taken by Astor's brother and relief that I'll never have to be in the same room as her again. I'm not sure which one of those is worse.

I shake my head at him, still trying to process the fact that he *killed* Ivan. "Why did you do it? Why did you even risk it?"

Astor takes a menacing step toward me, stealing whatever personal space I'd gained, and a dark storm-like look takes over his features. "Did you really just ask me why? You *know* why."

Tilting my chin, I boldly meet his intense gaze. "I want to hear you say it." He told me in the hospital that he'd hunt me down if I left, and now he's committed a serious crime for me. "Tell me why you did this."

"Because, against all logic and reason, you have found a way to completely ensnare me. Even if I wanted to try, I couldn't find a way to escape the web you've captured me in. You, Indie, have become the reason my heart beats, and the reason I wake up feeling lighter than I ever have." His hand gestures at the enclosure behind him. "I used to watch Periphas soar above me and found myself jealous of the freedom his wings allowed him. I'm not anymore because you've given me a type of freedom I didn't even know I desired." He reaches for me again and takes my face between his hands tenderly. "You've given me the freedom to smile and laugh, and you've given me the freedom to love."

"Astor..."

"I would risk everything I have for you, pretty girl, because I love you more than I thought possible. Before you, I truly didn't think I was capable of such a thing, and at the time, I was content with that. I was content going on with my life alone." He drops his forehead against mine and I close my eyes, adsorbing him and this moment. "But not anymore. Now I can't fathom you not being here with me, and that is why I couldn't allow someone who wanted to take you from me to remain alive."

My chest shudders with a shaky exhale as his thumbs sweep across my cheekbones.

"Do you understand now why I did what I did?" he questions. "And do you understand that I'd do it again without a second thought or moment of remorse. You're mine, Indie Riverton, and I will protect you as such."

"I understand." My fingers twist into the fabric of his shirt as I cling to him. "Thank you, Astor."

"Why on earth are you thanking me, baby?"

"Because I've forgotten what it's like to have someone who loves me," I admit, tilting my head back so I can look into his eyes. As usual, they look like they're full of thunderstorms. "So, thank you for reminding me and thank you for letting me love you back."

The corners of his mouth pull in a hint of a smile. "I'll remind you daily if you need me to." His hands trail down my body before hooking behind the back of my thighs. Without much effort, Astor lifts me from the ground and holds me up against him. "And I will *show* you just as often how much I love you."

Arms and legs looping around him, I tilt my head and kiss him gently. His touch is softer than I'm used to, and I know he's still being cautious because of my injury.

"Aren't you worried about what people will say about us on campus?" I ask, withdrawing back an inch.

While our relationship is sacred and special to us, it still might cause others to raise their brows and make unwanted remarks.

"No, I'm not worried," he assures me as he begins to carry me back toward the house. "People aren't idiotic enough to speak ill of someone with my last name. That's a guaranteed way for their lives to be ruined."

I don't doubt what he says for a second. He got away with disposing of Ivan, I'm certain he can get away with anything.

"But I don't have your last name."

Coming to a stop on the path that leads down to the dock, Astor kisses me again. "But you could," he murmurs against my lips.

"*What?*"

That devious smirk grows on his face, and I know whatever he's about to say is either going to make my heart explode in my chest or my pussy throb. It's a toss-up between the two, but they're *definitely* the only possibilities.

"What do you say, pretty girl? Want to enter another arrangement with me? But this one won't be just for eight months. I'm thinking of something a little more permanent and legally binding this time around." He skims his lips across my shocked parted ones. "It's a good deal. You'll get my last name and get to share my bed until death do us part."

Finally finding the ability to form words again, I ask him the same question that started all of this. "And what do you want in return?"

"You." His answer has the same effect on me as it did the first time he said it. "I'll only ever want you."

EPILOGUE
ASTOR

Five Months Later

I haven't seen a smile this big on her face since I asked her to marry me. That was a special day, but today is a triumphant day. Today is the first time Jupiter has allowed her to ride him since he was taken from her last summer. All the time and patience she put into helping him heal and regaining his trust have finally paid off. The relief she feels almost outshines her delight as she canters around the perimeter of the covered arena.

It's fucking freezing out and the sound of the pouring rain hitting the metal roof above us almost drowns out the sounds of her joyous laughs, but still, it's a really good day.

Eyes, the color of expensive scotch, find mine from across the arena and I smile encouragingly at her. She told me that I didn't have to be here today, but there wasn't a chance in hell I was letting her do this alone. She may be wearing a helmet and have been cleared by her doctors months ago, but the very thought of Jupiter throwing her off had icy fear running up my spine. Finding her unconscious in a hospital bed is something I'd like to only experience once in this lifetime.

To my delight, Jupiter, who has made leaps and bounds in his recovery, seems amazingly at ease today. The new barn we have him boarded at is smaller and offers him a calmer environment. The security updates the owner made also provide me with peace of mind when Indie is here alone. It also helps that any threats to her life have been taken care of. I haven't received an update on Indie's mother in while, but I'm sure Emeric is making her regret every breath she still takes. He has a way of doing that to people.

Footsteps crunching in the gravel have me turning my head away from the woman who's become everything to me. A dark figure walks toward the covered outdoor arena, the hood they wear over their head obscuring their face. If I hadn't been expecting him to show up, I would still be able to recognize him based on the scuffed boots on his feet.

Coming to a stop next to me on the opposite side of the arena fence I'm leaning on, Rafferty rests his elbows against the wood railing and silently watches Indie.

"Why am I here, Banes?" he asks after a tense moment of silence.

I don't bother greeting him as I turn my head back to Indie. Such polite gestures won't be necessary for this brief conversation. "I just thought you'd like to know that Posie Davenport's transfer application to Olympic Sound University has been accepted. She'll be starting in the performing arts program this fall."

I can feel his scrutinizing gaze on me. "Why did you follow through with it? Everyone already knows about your relationship since you ran off and married her."

At the mention of marriage, I twist the wedding band I swore I'd never wear around my finger. "Yes, but you're still privy to the more ... *distasteful* aspects of our relationship." Not for a second do I regret that our story started with a sinister arrangement. Frankly, I wouldn't change a damn thing about any of it. It played out exactly how it needed to for us to end up here. "Those are details that I would very much like to keep private."

"I see." Raffety nods. "So, getting Posie here ensures that those details die with me?"

Seeing as I've already made the necessary precautions to keep Cheska's mouth quiet, Rafferty is the only other person that could possibly be an issue.

I hesitate before answering, my eyes locked on the smile my wife wears. "Sometimes you have to make unsavory deals with the least likely of people to get what you really want."

"I'm out of here," he scoffs and takes a step away from the fence. "You sound like a fucking fortune cookie."

"Rafferty," I say lowly, stopping his retreat. "Can I give you some advice?"

"I think we both know that you're the last man I should be taking advice from, but if you really feel like wasting your time and breath, by all means, Banes, lay your words of wisdom upon me." His arms swoop in a mocking gesture, not a single fuck on his face or in his voice.

"You're graduating in a year, and when you do, you're set to inherit the reins of a very large corporation. It will require a level of responsibility and maturity that you've yet become accustomed too. My advice is that you take this next year and grow the fuck up. You will have a thousand people depending on you for their livelihood. For you to do what needs to be done, you're going to need to get these ploys, these *games* out of your system."

Like there's a violent storm rolling in, Rafferty's face darkens. His icy blue eyes become daggers as they narrow at me. "You don't think I know *responsibility*?" There's a calmness in his tone that shouldn't be there given his body language. "Are you forgetting that for the last five years, I've been doing everything *alone*? I was still a *kid* when they dumped it all on my lap, but somehow, I still figured it out. Not only have I kept myself going, but I've managed to keep my brother going as well. And we both know that hasn't been a small feat."

"What you've been through ... neither you nor your brother should have had to survive it." The events that took place in Rafferty's house five years ago were all people talked about for a year. Their heartache and misery became the town's entertainment.

"You're right, but we did, and it's *her* fault." A cold, menacing grin grows on his face, each of his wicked plans reflecting in it. "You said I play games, well, Banes, you've done me a great service and put my favorite player back on the board. Thank you for that."

Shaking my head, I sigh at the young man. "If this is really what you think you have to do to move on, then all I ask is you don't leave a blood trail on my campus."

"Fair enough."

He tips his chin and turns to walk away from me. I've just returned my attention to Indie when I hear him call my name again. "You're wrong about one thing though," he shouts back, not a care given that he's standing in the pouring rain. "I'm not just gaining responsibility next year, I'm gaining *resources. Unlimited* resources, in fact. My games aren't going to come to an end, they're only going to grow. They're going to extend past this fucking town and your campus, but in the meantime, I'm going to enjoy my reunion with Posie." Eyes flicking toward Indie, he adds, "Enjoy newlywed life, Banes."

With one last cocky lift of his lips and a mocking solute, Rafferty leaves, the dark cloud that's clung to him for five years lingering in his wake.

ALSO BY KAYLEIGH KING

The White Wolf Prophecy Series

Wolf Bound

Soul Bound

Shadow Bound

Fire Bound

The Crimson Crown Duet

Bloody Kingdom

Midnight Queen

Standalone Books

Catching Lightning

ACKNOWLEDGMENTS

First and foremost, I have to thank the readers for this one. This was my first venture into contemporary romance after spending a lot of time in the paranormal world. To say I was a nervous wreck for you guys to read this when it was first in Bully God is an understatement.

Your lovely reactions and reviews to the preview of Astor and Indie's story is what really pushed me to write the whole thing! Thank you for loving my words and stories, and for encouraging me to keep at it. I wouldn't be doing this without your endless support.

Cat: Oh my magical Kitchen (that's my nickname for her... IYKYK). I swear you can read my mind. You bring to life my visions even when I can't put them into words. Somehow you always just *know*. Working with you is probably my favorite part of this author journey. Love KK.

Greer: I don't know what to say that you don't already know. Every day I'm thankful that you were put in my life. You are my best friend and I can't imagine ever cowriting with someone else. Thank you for flying across the country and being my emotional-support friend at my first ever book signing. I'm not sure I would have gone if you hadn't agreed to be there for me. I can't wait to see what else we can create together.

Aundi: My love, my fucking, love. Your messages while beta reading this story made me excited to release it. On those days when I was doubting myself and you took the time to talk me off the ledge, I'm so grateful for you.

Bre: I don't know how you made time to beta read for me with your crazy mom schedule. You are a super star. Thank you for loving Astor as much as I do. I know you said you licked him so he's yours, but I suspect you may have to fight off some people for him. Good luck, boo.

Christina: Thank you for holding down the fort so I can disappear into my writing cave. Also thank you for letting me slide into your DMs with my complete and utter nonsense all the time. I don't know why you put up with me.

Ellie & Rosa: If you wanted to fire me as a client, I wouldn't even blame you. The deadlines I put you on are cruel, but thank you nonetheless, for always working with me. Thank you for making my words pretty.

ABOUT THE AUTHOR

USA Today Bestselling author Kayleigh King is a writer of contemporary and paranormal romance. She creates love stories that will stick with you, almost like they're haunting you. She's a Diet Coke and cold brew addict, sharing music is her love language, and she seriously lacks a filter. Anything she thinks, she usually says. And if she doesn't say it, her facial expressions will say it for her. Currently residing in Denver Colorado, you'll never find her on a snowboard since she avoids the snow like the plague.

Want to chat about books, music, or life in general? Make sure you join her Facebook reader group and follow her on Instagram. Her DMs are always open to her readers.

- instagram.com/kayleighkingwrites
- facebook.com/kayleighkingwrites
- tiktok.com/@kayleighkingauthor
- amazon.com/author/kayleighkingwrites
- goodreads.com/kayleighkingwrites

Made in the USA
Middletown, DE
03 July 2022